STILETTO

HAROLD ROBBINS

The scorching story of a man no woman could resist and no man could rival . . . a man equally at home in the elegant palaces of European aristocracy, in the opulent penthouses of New York's power elite, and in the secret backroom meeting places of the Mafia bosses. A man no one could touch . . . except the one woman who had the power to destroy him.

STILETTO

HAROLD ROBBINS

A DELL BOOK

Published by
Dell Publishing Co., Inc.
1 Dag Hammarskjold Plaza
New York, New York 10017

This is a work of fiction, and all characters and events in
the story are fictional, and any resemblance to real
persons is purely coincidental.

Dell ® TM 681510, Dell Publishing Co., Inc.

ISBN: 0-440-18284-0

Printed in the United States of America
Three Previous Editions
New Edition
First printing—March 1982
Seventh printing—November 1984

1

It was after ten o'clock and there were only three men at the bar and one man at a table in the rear when the hustler came in. A blast of the cold night air came in with her.

She climbed up on a stool and let her thin winter coat fall from her shoulders. "Gimme a beer," she said.

Silently the bartender drew a glass of beer and placed it in front of her. He picked up the quarter and rang it up.

"Any action tonight, Jimmy?" she asked, her eyes searching the men at the bar for a response to her question.

The bartender shook his head. "Not tonight, Maria. It's Sunday night and all the *touristas* are home in their beds." He walked away and began to polish some glasses under the bar. He watched her sip at her beer. Maria. He called them all Maria. The little Puerto Rican girls with their bright shiny black eyes and their hard little breasts and buttocks. He wondered when she had had her last shot.

The hustler gave up on the men at the bar. She turned to look at the man seated at the table. She could only see his back but she could tell from the cut of his clothing that he wasn't local. She looked questioningly at the bartender. He shrugged his shoulders and she slid off her stool and started back to the table.

The man was looking down at his whisky glass when she stopped beside him. "Lonesome, señor?" she asked.

She knew the moment he lifted his head to look at her what his answer would be. The dark ice-blue eyes and tanned face and hungry mouth. Men such as he never bought their pleasures, they took them.

"No, thank you," Cesare said politely.

The hustler smiled vaguely, nodded her head and went back to the bar. She climbed up on the stool again and took out a cigarette.

The stocky little bartender held a match for her. "Like I said," he whispered, smiling, "it's Sunday night."

The girl dragged deep on the cigarette and let the smoke out slowly. "I know," she said tonelessly, the first faint sign of worry appearing on her face. "But I gotta keep workin'. It's an expensive habit."

The telephone in the booth beside the bar began to ring and the bartender left her to answer it. He came out of the booth and walked over to Cesare's table. *"Para usted, señor."*

STILETTO

"Mil gracias," Cesare answered, going to the telephone. "Hello," he said as he closed the door of the booth.

The woman's voice was almost a whisper. She spoke in Italian. "It will have to be in the morning," she said, "before he appears in court."

Cesare answered in the same language. "There is no other place?"

"No," she said, her voice very clear in the receiver despite its softness. "We have not been able to learn where he is coming from. We only know that he will appear at court at eleven o'clock."

"And the others?" Cesare asked. "Are they still in the same place?"

"Yes," she answered. "In Las Vegas and Miami. Are your plans made?"

"I have everything in readiness," Cesare replied.

The woman's voice grew harsh. "The man must die before he sits in the witness chair. The others too."

Cesare laughed shortly. "Tell Don Emilio not to worry. They are all as good as dead right now."

He put down the telephone and walked out into the dark Spanish Harlem night. He turned his collar up against the cold winter wind and began to walk. Two blocks away on Park Avenue he caught a lone cruising taxi. He climbed into it. "El Morocco," he said to the driver.

He sank back into his seat and lit a cigarette, an excitement beginning inside him. It was real now. For the first time since the war it was real again. He remembered how it was the first time. The first girl and the first death. Strange how they always seemed to

7

come together. The reality of living was never greater than when you held death clutched tightly in your hands.

It seemed a long time ago. He was fifteen years old and the year was 1935. There had been a parade in the little Sicilian village at the foot of the mountain that day. The Fascisti were always having parades. There were banners and pictures of Il Duce everywhere. His scowling face and angry clenched fist and piglike bulging eyes. Live Dangerously. Be Italian. Italy Means Strength.

It had been evening when Cesare reached the foot of the mountain on his way home. He looked up. The castle stood there on the edge of a promontory near the peak. Ornate and ugly. As it had been for almost six hundred years. Since some long-gone ancestor, the first Count Cardinali, took to wife a daughter of the family Borgia.

He had started up the mountain past Gandolfo's vineyard and the heavy smell of the black grapes came out to him. He could still remember the drums beating and the excitement inside him that night. His mind was filled with the old recruiting sergeant's lewd stories of the orgies that took place in Il Duce's palace.

"*Collones!*" the old soldier had chortled. "There never was such *collones* in all the history of Italy! Five different girls he had in one night. I know for it was my duty to bring each one of them to him. And each girl left bowlegged, as if she had been mounted by a bull. While he, he was up at six o'clock in the morning, strong and fresh, leading us in two hours of drill." The spittle ran down his cheeks. "I tell you, young fellows, if it's women you want, the uniform of the Italian Army will get them for you. It makes every girl think she's getting a piece of Il Duce!"

It was then that Cesare had seen the girl. She had come from in back of the Gandolfo house. He had seen her before but never when his senses had been so aflame. She was a tall, strong, full-breasted animal, this daughter of the wine-maker, and she was carrying a skin of wine from the cooling house in the back field near the stream. She paused when she saw him.

He stopped and looked at her. The heat of the day was still heavy in him and he wiped the beads of sweat from his face with the back of his arm.

Her voice was very soft and respectful. "Perhaps the signor would like a drink of cooling wine?"

He nodded, not speaking, and walked toward her. He held the skin high and the red wine ran down his throat, spilling over his chin. He felt the grape bite into him and warm him inside and cool him at the same time. He gave the skin back to her and they stood there looking at each other.

Slowly a redness crept up from her throat and bosom into her face and her eyes fell. He could see the sudden thrusting of her nipples against the thin peasant blouse and the swell of her breasts over the top of it.

He turned away from her and began to walk into the woods. From the generations of knowledge deep inside him came the command that had no doubt about its ability to possess.

"Come!"

Obediently, almost as if she were an automaton, the girl followed him. Deep into the woods where the trees were so thick one could hardly see the sky above.

She sank to the ground beside him and never said a word while his fingers stripped the clothing from her body.

He knelt there for a moment, studying the strong muscular lines of her body, the full plum-tipped breasts, the flat muscular belly that rose and fell, her heavy strong legs. He felt a torrent rise inside him and he threw himself across her.

It was the first time for him but not for her. Twice he screamed in an agony as she locked him tightly to her then, spent, he rolled away and lay breathing heavily on the moist ground beside her.

She turned toward him silently, her fingers and mouth exploring, probing. At first he pushed her away, then his hands touched her breasts and froze there. Involuntarily he squeezed and she cried out in pain.

For the first time now he looked into her face. Her eyes were wide and moisture was full in them. He squeezed again. Again she cried out. But this time her eyes were closed. There were tears in their corners but her mouth was open in a gasping ecstasy as if she sought to gulp strength from the air.

A sense of power he had never known before came up in him. Cruelly now, he tightened his fingers. This time her scream of pain sent the birds shrilling from the perches in the trees. Her eyes flew open and she stared at him, then worshipfully she bent her head to his suddenly reawakened body.

It was dark when he began to walk away from her. He felt strong and complete and the grass was like carpet beneath his feet. He was almost at the edge of the small clearing when her voice stopped him.

"Signor!"

He turned around. She was on her feet now and her nude body gleamed in the dark as if it sprang from the very earth itself. Her eyes were luminous pools in her face. She half smiled to herself, a pride and satisfaction deep within her. The others would be jealous when she told them of this. This was no laborer, no itinerant crop worker. This was the blood, the true blood, the future Count Cardinali.

"Grazia!" she said sincerely.

He nodded curtly and plunged into the woods and was gone from her sight before she could bend to pick up her clothing.

It was six weeks later at the fencing school down in the village that Cesare next heard of her. The Maestro had long since given up teaching Cesare who was far superior to his ageing skills and only attended classes to keep in practice. The door had opened and a young soldier entered.

He came into the small gymnasium and looked around, his modern Il Ducc's guard uniform oddly out of place in this ancient atmosphere of swords. His voice was tense. "Which one of you is known by the name of Cesare Cardinali?"

There was a sudden silence in the room. The two young men who were fencing put down their foils and turned to the newcomer. Cesare came slowly from the wall where he had been practicing with the weights.

He stopped in front of the soldier. "I am," he said.

The soldier stared at him. "I am the affianced of my cousin, Rosa," he said tightly.

Cesare looked at him. He knew no one by that name. "And who is she?" he asked politely.

"Rosa Gandolfo!" The name tore angrily from the

11

soldier's lips. "And I am called from my post in Rome to marry her because you have made her with child!"

Cesare stared at him for a moment as the understanding came to him. Then he relaxed slightly. "Is that all?" he asked, a strange feeling of pride beginning to come up inside him. "I will speak to my father, the Count, about some money for you."

He turned and started to walk away. The soldier spun him around again. "Money?" he shouted. "Is that all you think I want? Money? No!"

Cesare looked at him coldly. "As you wish. Then I will not speak with my father."

The soldier's hand slashed across his face. "I demand satisfaction!"

The handprint stood out clearly on Cesare's suddenly white face. He stared at the soldier without fear. "The Cardinalis find no honor in fighting with a commoner."

The soldier spat forth the words venomously: "The Cardinalis are cowards, pimps and despoilers of women! And you, the bastard son, are more like them than they are themselves! Il Duce was right when he said that the aristocrats of Italy are sick and decadent and that they must give way to the strength of the paisanos!"

Cesare's hand moved faster than light and, though the soldier weighed a good twenty pounds more than he, the soldier sprawled on the floor. Cesare looked down at him. A strange look began to come into his face, his eyes grew dark, so dark one could not see the blue of them. He looked up at the Maestro. It had been a long time since anyone had dared refer to his illegitimate birth.

"Give him a sword," he said quietly. "I will fight him."

"No, Signor Cesare, no!" The Maestro was frightened. "The Count, your father, will not—"

Cesare interrupted him. His voice was quiet but there was no mistaking the authority in it. "Give him a sword. My father will not like this slur on our name to go unanswered!"

The soldier was on his feet now. He smiled and looked at Cesare. "In the army of Italy we are trained in the tradition. A sword in the right hand, a stiletto in the left."

Cesare nodded. "So be it."

The soldier began to take off his jacket, his muscular arms and shoulders came into view. He stared confidently at Cesare. "Send for a priest, my young rapist," he said, "for you are already a dead man."

Cesare did not answer, but deep in his eyes an unholy joy began to grow. He threw his shirt on the floor. "Ready?"

The soldier nodded. The Maestro called position. Cesare's white frame looked thin beside the heavy brown body of the soldier.

"En garde!"

The crossed swords gleamed over their heads. The Maestro struck them up. The soldier's sword flashed down in a powerful thrust.

Cesare parried and the sword slipped past his side. He laughed aloud. The soldier cursed and slashed heavily. Lightly Cesare slid the blow away from him and bent to the attack. Quickly he circled his foil, the swords locked and he tore the soldier's sword from his grasp. It fell clattering to the floor.

13

Cesare placed his sword's point against the soldier's breast. "Your honor, sir?"

The soldier cursed and struck it away with his stiletto. He circled to one side trying to get to his sword but Cesare was in front of him.

The soldier stared at him and cursed. Cesare laughed again. There was a joy in him now that none there had ever seen. Cesare threw his sword into the corner beside the other.

Before its clatter ceased the soldier sprang at him, the stiletto flashing downward toward Cesare's face. Cesare moved slightly and the stiletto slashed the empty air.

Cesare was crouching, the stiletto held lightly, point out, in the palm of his hand. The soldier, too, was crouching now. Warily he reached out. Cesare easily parried.

Cesare thrust forward; the soldier stepped back then, seeing an opening, sprang again. This time the two bodies locked in a grotesque embrace. Cesare seemed all but lost as the soldier's arms wrapped themselves around him. They stood there for a moment, swaying back and forth as if in some obscene embrace, then slowly the soldier's arms began to fall.

His stiletto fell from his nerveless fingers and he sank to his knees on the floor, his hands clutching at Cesare's hips. Cesare stepped back.

It was then they could see the stiletto in Cesare's hand.

The soldier fell face down on the floor and the Maestro hurriedly rushed forward. "Call a doctor!" he said anxiously, kneeling beside the soldier.

STILETTO

Cesare turned from picking up his shirt. "Don't bother," he said quietly, starting for the door. "He's dead."

Unthinking, he dropped the stiletto in his jacket as he went out the door into the night.

The girl was waiting for him on the hill where the road made its last turn toward the castle. He stopped when he saw her. They stared at each other silently. Then Cesare turned and walked off the road into the woods. Obediently the girl followed him.

When they could no longer see the road, Cesare turned to her. Her eyes were wide and luminous as she stepped toward him. He ripped down her blouse and seized her naked breasts cruelly in his hands.

"Ai-ee!" she screamed, half fainting.

Then the pain tore through him, from his swollen testes to his vitals. Frantically he ripped his clothing from him, his seed already spilling wildly on the ground.

The bright Sicilian moon was already high over their heads when he sat up in the darkness and reached for his clothing.

"Signor," she whispered.

He didn't answer. His hands found his trousers and he got up and stepped into them.

"Signor, I have come to warn you. My cousin—"

"I know," he interrupted, looking down at her.

Her voice was frightened. "But he said he was going to kill you."

He laughed almost silently. "I am here."

"But, signor, he may find you any moment. Even here. He is very jealous and very proud."

15

"Not any more," Cesare said flatly. "He is dead."

"Dead?" The girl's voice was almost a scream. She leaped to her feet. "You killed him?"

Cesare was buttoning his shirt. "*Si,*" he said shortly.

She came at him like a tigress, her hands scratching and striking at him. She was half crying, half screaming. "You fiend! Lie with me when his blood is still fresh on your hands? Lower than animals, you! Who am I to marry now? What am I going to do with this thing you put in my belly?"

A sudden knowledge came to him as he gripped her hands and held them tight. "You wanted it there or it wouldn't be there," he said.

She stared up into his eyes knowing now that he knew. She drew her head back and spat up into his face. "I don't want it now!" she shouted. "It will be a monster, a bastard like its father!"

He brought his knee up sharply into the softness of her belly. The pain choked in her throat and she fell, writhing and vomiting against the earth.

He looked down at her, his hand involuntarily going into his jacket pocket and finding the stiletto still there. He took it out.

She looked up at him, a fear beginning to grow in her eyes.

His lips pulled back in a cold smile. "If you don't want it then, cut it out of yourself with this." He threw the stiletto to the ground beside her. "It will purify you. His blood is still on it."

He turned and walked away.

In the morning they found the girl dead. She was lying there with the stiletto grasped in her two hands, her thighs already caked with the drying blood that had soaked into the earth beneath her.

Two days later Cesare left for school in England. He was not to return to Italy until the war began almost five years later.

In the meantime the Gandolfos built a new winery with the ten thousand lire Count Cardinali gave them.

The taxi pulled to a stop before El Morocco and the giant doorman opened the door. He saw Cesare and smiled. "Ah, Count Cardinali," he said warmly. "Good evening. I was beginning to think we weren't going to see you tonight."

Cesare paid the driver and got out of the taxi, looking at his watch. It was eleven-thirty. He smiled to himself. The thought of the woman waiting inside the restaurant for him was part of the excitement too. Her warm lovely body also held the reality of living.

2

Special Agent George Baker began to turn off the lights in his office. When he reached the door he hesitated a moment, then went back to his desk and picked up the telephone. It was a direct line to Captain Strang at Police Headquarters. "How does it look?" Baker asked.

Strang's heavy voice boomed through the wire. "Haven't you gone home yet? It's after eleven o'clock."

"I know," Baker replied. "I had some things to clean up. I thought I'd check with you before I left."

"There's nothing to worry about," the policeman boomed confidently. "We got the place covered. The area around the courthouse is clear and I put men in every building and on every corner all around the place. They will stay there all night and through the morning until we get the witness into court. Believe me, nobody will get within ten feet of him until he enters the courthouse."

"Good," Baker said. "I'll go right out to the airport in the morning and meet the plane. I'll see you at the courthouse at eleven o'clock."

"Okay. Stop worrying now and get some sleep," Strang said. "Everything's under control here."

But when Baker got back to his hotel room, he couldn't sleep. He sat up in bed and thought of calling his wife, then put the thought out of his mind. She would be too upset at the telephone call in the middle of the night. He got out of bed and sat in a chair.

Idly he took his gun from the holster draped over the back of the chair and checked it. He spun the cylinder and thrust it back in the holster. I'm edgy, he thought. I've been on this thing too long.

For the past six years there had been nothing else for him. Only this one case. "Break the back of the Mafia, the Society, the Syndicate, or whatever the name of the organization is that has a stranglehold on America's underworld," the chief had said to him.

He was a young man then, at least it seemed so because he felt like an old man now. When he had started on this case, his son had been a junior in high school; this year the boy was graduating from college.

Time went by; the years had passed frustratingly as every lead petered out. There was no way to get to the top, to the Dons. Sure, the small fry kept falling into their traps with almost statistical regularity; but the big ones always got away.

Then the break had come. A man had talked about the murder of two federal narcotics agents aboard a

STILETTO

small ship just coming into New York. Painstakingly the lead had been followed and now for the first time in the history of organized crime, four of its top leaders were on trial. For murder and conspiracy to murder.

In his mind's eye he could see the I.D. file on each defendant. George "Big Dutch" Wehrman, age 57, 21 arrests, no convictions, present occupation union official; Allie "The Fixer" Fargo, age 56, 1 arrest, 1 conviction, 1 suspended sentence, present occupation contractor; Nicholas "Dandy Nick" Pappas, age 54, 32 arrests, 9 for murder, 2 convictions, 20 days in jail, present occupation none, known gambler; Emilio "The Judge" Matteo, age 61, 11 arrests, 1 conviction, 5 years in jail, deported, present occupation retired.

The thought of the last man brought a bitter smile to his lips. Retired, the report had said. Retired from what? From murder, from narcotics, from participation in almost any form of illegal activity conceived by the mind of man? Not the Judge, not Don Emilio as he was sometimes called by his associates.

Deportation to Italy along with Luciano and Adonis after the war had resulted only in giving him a license to steal. No matter what aid Matteo had given the government in planning the invasion of Italy during the war, they should not have agreed to let him out of jail. Once they had a man like that locked up, the only sensible thing to do was to throw away the key.

Baker remembered the countless times he had gone flying around the country on the tip that Matteo had come back; but he was never there. Still there were all the signs that he had been there. The narcotics and the dead. Mute evidence. But this time it was different.

21

This time they had evidence that would talk, if only to save their own lives. And because of that evidence, Matteo had been brought back from Italy.

It had taken a long time but now they had them. Three witnesses, whose testimony corroborated each other. The testimony that almost certainly meant death for the defendants. There was only one problem remaining now. That was to bring each man to the witness chair in the courtroom—alive.

Restlessly Baker got out of the chair and walked over to the window and stared out at the darkened city. Knowing Matteo as he did, he was certain that somewhere out there, somewhere in the city, an assassin or assassins were waiting.

The big questions were how, what, when, where and who?

The maitre d' with the mustache bowed obsequiously before her. "Miss Lang," he murmured, "Count Cardinali is already here. If you will follow me, please."

He turned and she followed him with her slow, graceful, model's walk, her long red tresses shimmering against her shoulders. She walked slowly, savoring the turning heads, the appreciative looks following her. She heard one of the dowagers whispering.

"That's the 'Smoke and Flame' girl, Barbara Lang. You know, my dear. From the cosmetic ads."

The captain led her down along the zebra-striped banquette to where Cesare sat at a table. Cesare rose as he saw her. He smiled and kissed her hand as the captain held the table away. She sat down and let her coat slip back on the banquette.

"Champagne?" Cesare asked.

She nodded as she looked around the restaurant. The soft lights, the elaborately jeweled women and the men with the round, well-fed, yet hungry faces. This was the heights. This was El Morocco. And she was here with a real Count. Not with a phony, half-slobbering promoter who sat with one hand holding in his fat little gut and the other hand under the table trying to creep up inside her dress.

She turned to look at him as she lifted the glass to her lips. Cesare, Count Cardinali, who could trace his family back six hundred years to the time of the Borgias, who drove racing cars all over the world, who had his name in the society columns every day.

"Will you be ready in the morning?" he asked, smiling.

She returned his smile. "I'm very efficient," she said. "My bags are already packed."

"Good," he nodded, lifting his glass. "To you."

"To our holiday." She smiled. She sipped her champagne reflectively. It hadn't always been like this. It wasn't too long ago that the only "sparkling" drink she had tasted was beer. It seemed only the day before yesterday that the model school she had attended while working as a clerk in the store back home in Buffalo had called her. There was a chance for her to get some work and experience doing some publicity on a motion picture that was having its première locally.

She had taken the afternoon off and gone up to the hotel for an interview. Nervously she stood in the corridor outside the largest suite in the hotel and heard the raucous shouts of laughter coming from inside the suite. Quickly, before she lost her nerve, she pressed the buzzer. The door opened and a tall young man stood there.

She took a deep breath and the words tumbled out. "I'm Barbara Lang," she said. "The agency sent me over. They said you needed a girl for publicity work."

The young man stood there for a moment and looked at her. Then he smiled. It was a pleasant smile and gave his rather pale face a nice, gentle look. He stepped back and opened the door wide. "I'm Jed Goliath," he said. "I handle the publicity. Come on in, I'll introduce you around."

She had entered the room, hoping her nervousness wouldn't show. She felt the moisture breaking out on her upper lip the way it always did and silently she cursed to herself. There were three other men in the living room of the suite and a table set up in the corner held the makings of a cocktail lounge.

Goliath led her over to the man seated on a chair near the open window. Despite his smile, his face had a tortured, worried look. This was Mendel Bayliss, the writer-producer of the picture, and the worried look came from having his own money in the picture. "Hi," he said. "Its hot. Have a drink?"

The second man was one she recognized right away. He was the second banana on a weekly television show. The pratfall kid they called him. He had just stopped by to visit the producer for whom he had worked in an unsuccessful show some years before.

The third man was Johnny Gleason. He was the local manager of the motion-picture company. He was tall, red-faced and very drunk. He stood up and bowed when they were introduced and almost fell over the coffee table in front of him.

Jed smiled at Barbara encouragingly as he pushed the manager safely back on the couch. "We've been drinking since eight o'clock this morning," he explained.

She managed a smile as if to imply that things like this happened every day in her life. "The agency said there was some publicity work to do on a movie," she said, trying to get some note of business back into the meeting.

"That's right," Jed answered. "We need a Never-Never girl."

"A what?" she gasped.

"A Never-Never girl," he explained. "That's the name of our picture. 'Never, Never.'"

"You're tall," Bayliss said.

"Five-nine," she answered.

"Take off your shoes," he answered, standing up.

She took off her shoes and stood there holding them in her hand while he walked over and stood next to her.

"I'm five-eleven," he said proudly. "We can't have a girl taller than me in all the newspaper pictures. You'll have to wear low heels."

"Yes, sir," she said.

He walked back to his chair and sat down, his eyes going over her figure appraisingly. "Bring a bathing suit with you?" he asked.

She nodded. It was standard equipment in the model's hatbox she carried with her everywhere she went.

"Put it on," he said curtly. "Let's see what you got."

The pratfall kid picked it right up. He weaved his way over to her and peered up into her face. He leered happily. "We won't mind if you show us without the bathing suit either, baby," he whispered loudly.

She could feel her face flushing and she looked helplessly at Jed. He smiled again reassuringly and led her to a bedroom. "You can change in here," he said, closing the door behind her.

She changed swiftly, pausing only for a moment to check herself in the bathroom mirror. For once she was grateful for the golden tan that clung to her since the summer. She took a Kleenex and patted the moisture from her upper lip and went back into the living room.

All eyes turned to her as she opened the door. For a moment she felt self-conscious, then with her model's walk she glided to the center of the room and slowly turned around.

"She's got a good clean figure," the producer said.

"Not enough tits for me," the pratfall kid chortled. "I'm a T-man, myself."

The producer was still watching her. "What d'yuh expect from a high-fashion model? The clothes fall better on them without 'em. She's got more than most." He looked up at her face. "Thirty-five?" he asked.

She nodded.

The producer got to his feet, smiling. "I got the best eye in Hollywood," he said. "Haven't guessed wrong in twenty years." He turned to Jed. "She'll do."

The pratfall kid came over and leered up at her breasts. "Thanks for the mammaries," he sang in an off-key voice.

26

Bayliss laughed. "Cut the clownin'," he said. "Come on, it's time we got something to eat." He started for the door.

The pratfall kid and the film manager staggered after him to the door. At the door Bayliss turned back and spoke to Jed. "Tell her what she's gotta do and have her at the press conference at five o'clock."

The door closed behind them and she and Jed looked at each other. He smiled. "Maybe you'd like to sit down for a moment and catch your breath?"

Her legs felt suddenly weak. She smiled gratefully and sank into the chair the producer had vacated. It was still warm from his body.

Jed filled a glass with ice cubes and poured a bottle of Coke into it. He took it over and handed it to her.

"Thanks," she said, taking it from him and sipping it.

"They're crazy," he said, still smiling, looking down at her white bathing suit and her long tan legs.

"Are they always like that?" she asked.

Jed was still smiling but she thought she detected a faint note of bitterness in his voice. "Always," he answered. "They're big men. They're always proving something."

For the next week she was the best-known girl in Buffalo. Not a day passed that her picture wasn't in the papers. Twice that week she was in the Niagara Falls paper. She was on every local radio and television show and met every important newspaperman and person in the area.

Jed was always near. Unobtrusively he set up pictures for her and the producer, together and alone. Somewhere in the picture was always a plug for the movie. That first night she didn't get home until three o'clock in the morning. The next night she didn't get home at all. She spent the night in Jed's room.

It was a giddy, supercharged week and when it was over, everything seemed flat and meaningless. Of all the people she had met that week, no one seemed to remember her, not even the matrons who attended the weekly fashion show at the department store where she worked.

She remembered what Jed had said to her the last night. "You got too much for this hick town, Barbara. You come down to New York. That's the place for a girl like you."

He had given her his card and the card of a photographer he knew. Six months later she went to New York. The manager of Jed's building said that he had moved to California but the photographer was still there. The funny thing about it all was that Jed had been right. New York *was* the place for her. Within two weeks she had an assignment for a *Vogue* cover. Within a year she was one of the most sought-after high-fashion models in New York. Her fee was sixty dollars an hour and she earned almost twenty thousand a year.

She worked very hard and went out very little. The camera was too harsh and revealing when she did not get enough rest. On the weekends she flew home to Buffalo and lounged around the front yard of the new house she had bought for her mother.

Then one afternoon she had been modeling some new suits in front of the Plaza Hotel. One of the props they were using was a bright red, Alfa-Romeo sports car. As she posed opening the door of the car, the agency executive came up to her. With him was a tall, lean, foreign-looking man. The man had a handsome, savage look about him and when he smiled his teeth were strong and white.

"Barbara," the agency executive said, "I'd like you to meet Count Cardinali. He was kind enough to loan us this car for these shots."

Barbara looked up at him. She knew the name. Count Cardinali. It was one of those names you read in the papers. Almost a legend. Like De Portago and Pignatari, somehow you never expected them to be quite real.

Cesare took her hand and kissed it. "So pleased to meet you." He smiled.

She smiled and nodded and he went away and she went back to work. That evening she was lounging in her slacks, watching television, when the phone rang. She picked it up. "Hello," she said.

"Barbara?" Somehow his accent was slightly stronger when it came through the telephone. "This is Cesare Cardinali. How would you like to have some supper with me tonight?"

"I—I don't know," she answered, unexpectedly flustered. "I was just lounging around."

His voice was very sure. "That's all right. I won't pick you up until eleven o'clock. We'll go to El Morocco."

He put down the phone before she could answer and she went into the bathroom and began drawing a tub of water. It wasn't until she was in the steaming tub that she realized she was really going to see him that night.

Later, when they were seated in the restaurant, he

29

lifted his glass of champagne toward her. "Barbara," he said in a serious voice. "There is a great deal of talk around town that you are planning to become a promiscuous woman. I like that. And I would like it even more if you would allow me to be of some help in that matter."

"What?" she gasped, looking at him startled.

But he was smiling and she knew that he was mocking her. She began to smile and picked up her glass. He had a lot to learn about American girls.

Now Cesare's voice brought her back from her reverie. "I'll pick you up about nine-thirty," he was saying. "That will give me time to go down to the courthouse and get my papers before we drive to the airport."

"Fine," she said. "I'll be ready."

3

Cesare pulled the red Alfa-Romeo into a parking place outside the building reserved for official cars only. He grinned at Barbara. "You don't mind waiting a few minutes while I run inside and pick up the papers, do you?"

She shook her head. But with a typical middle-class fear of official signs and orders, she said, "Hurry, I don't want them to chase me out of here."

"They won't," Cesare said confidently, getting out of the car. He walked toward the building, his Alpine fedora sitting jauntily on his head.

She looked after him as he went into the entrance. He walked under the sign that read *U. S. Dept. of Immigration and Naturalization* and disappeared into the building. In some ways he was like a small boy.

That was how it had been when he called her up last

week. He had just returned from Europe, he had said, and had visited his home. Now his mind was made up. He was going to become an American citizen. And to celebrate it, when he picked up the papers, would she join him on a week's vacation some place where the sun was shining?

She had agreed to go without even thinking about it but when she put down the telephone she began to smile to herself. Maybe this time he was serious about a girl. Of course she had heard about the others but a whole week— A lot could happen in a week.

There was a noise from around the corner and she looked up. There seemed to be a crowd of people gathering there. A policeman came by. He stopped at the side of the car and looked at her. "Will you be here long, miss?" he asked.

"Not long, officer," she said quickly. "My friend just went inside to pick up his first papers."

The policeman nodded and started to walk away. A roar came from around the corner. She called after him. "What's going on around the corner, officer?"

He glanced toward the corner and then back at her. "That's Foley Square, miss. They're starting the big trial of them gangsters this morning. It seems like everybody in New York wants to get into that court-room."

Cesare went into the first reception room. The clerk at the counter looked up at him. "I'm Cesare Cardinali," he said. "I've come to pick up my papers."

The clerk nodded. "First papers?"

"Yes," Cesare answered.

STILETTO

The clerk checked a tab file on the counter. He pulled out a small card and looked up. "If you'll just take a seat, Mr. Cardinali, I'll have them ready for you in about ten minutes."

Cesare smiled. "That will be fine." He hesitated a moment then asked, "Is there a lavatory around here?"

The clerk smiled and pointed out the door. "Down the hall to your left," he said.

"Thank you," Cesare answered, already on his way to the door. "I'll be right back."

He walked out the door and down the hall. He stopped in front of the men's room and looked around. There was no one watching. He walked quickly past it and opened a door marked, *stairs*. The door closed behind him and he began to go up the steps two at a time.

The black limousine pulled to a stop in front of the courthouse and the crowd pressed around it. Baker looked out from his seat next to the witness then turned back to him. "You're a big draw," he said.

Dinky Adams, the witness, a long horse-faced man, shrank back in his seat and pulled his hat down over his face. "Big deal," he snarled humorlessly. "My life ain't goin' to be worth two cents once they know who I am."

"Nobody's going to bother you," Baker said reassuringly. "We told you you would be protected and we've done all right so far."

A flying squad of police cleared the area around the car. Captain Strang stuck his head down near the window. "Okay, let's go."

Baker got out first, followed by three other agents. They stood there for a moment looking around, then Baker nodded and the witness began to get out.

A roar of recognition came up from the crowd. The agents and police crowded in around him as they started to move through the mass. Photographers and reporters were yelling questions at them but they kept moving on up the steps, entered the courthouse and moved down the corridor.

"This way," Strang said. "We've got an elevator waiting."

They followed the police captain into an empty elevator. The doors were promptly closed and the car started up. Intangibly the tension seemed to disappear. Baker looked at Strang. "Well, we made it," he said, smiling.

The policeman nodded and smiled back at him. "The worst is over. All we got to get through upstairs is the reporters."

Dinky looked at them. His face was white and still frightened. "I got time the rest of my life to congratulate you guys. If I live long enough."

The smile disappeared from Baker's face. The detectives looked at one another and then turned seriously toward the door as it began to open.

Cesare came out of the stairway on the third floor and turned and pushed his way quickly toward the elevators. He looked across the crowd to the courtroom doors. There were two policemen standing there. He pulled his right hand up into the sleeve of his lined car coat and felt the cold metal of the stiletto tingle against his fingers. A strange smile began to come to his lips.

He could feel his heart beginning to thump inside his chest. It was the way he felt when he took a car into a tight curve and didn't know whether he had enough traction to make it. He took a deep breath and the smile became fixed on his face.

The elevator door opened and the crowd surged toward it. Cesare didn't move. He knew they wouldn't be on that car. His information was complete. It was just too bad that he hadn't more time to prepare. He leaned back against the wall between the second and third elevators.

The next door opened and the detectives came out in a phalanx around the witness. Cesare stepped in quickly behind them and let the crowd push him along. There was no chance for him here, a detective was between him and the witness. The reporters were screaming unanswered questions. Flashbulbs were going off as the photographers jumped up and down trying to get a picture of the witness. He could only hope for a break. Once the man got into the courtroom it would be too late.

They were near the door now and the stiletto was cold in Cesare's hand. He had stopped breathing a long time ago. His lungs were filled to bursting with oxygen that would never be needed. There was a heavy pressure in his ears and everyone seemed to be moving in a sort of slow motion.

The group stopped for a moment before the closed door. The detective behind the witness moved slightly. The air spilled from Cesare's lungs in a gasp. The crowd pushed against his back, thrusting him forward. Now! Now was the time!

Cesare never even felt his hand move. It was almost as if it weren't even a part of him. The stiletto slid into the witness's heart as easily as a warm knife into butter. Cesare felt the blade snap back into his sleeve, pulled by the coiled wire attached to its hilt, as he opened his palm.

The witness stumbled slightly as the two policemen moved to open the door to the courtroom. Cesare began to walk toward the stairway. A flashbulb went off almost in his face, momentarily blinding him, but then his vision cleared and he kept on walking.

There was a hush in the courtroom. From outside in the corridor they could hear some noise growing. The sound of voices grew louder.

Matteo looked at the other defendants. Big Dutch was playing nervously with his tie clasp, Allie Fargo was tearing at his nails with his fingers, even Dandy Nick was doodling on the yellow pad before him. The noise grew louder.

Big Dutch leaned over toward him. "I wonder who they bringin' in," he said.

Dandy Nick grinned. It was an unhealthy grin of fear. "You'll find out soon enough," he said.

Matteo shut them up with a gesture, his eyes watching the courtroom door. The others turned to look.

First a couple of detectives appeared in the doorway, then the witness. He stumbled for a moment and a cop put out a hand to steady him.

Big Dutch leaped to his feet with an angry roar. "It's Dinky Adams, the son of a bitch!"

STILETTO

The judge's gavel rapped on the desk. The witness took several more steps into the courtroom. His face seemed to be glazed with fear. He stumbled again. He looked down the courtroom toward the defendants' table. He opened his mouth as if to speak but no sound came out. Only a tiny dribble of blood appeared in the corner of his lips. A tortured look came into his eyes and he stumbled again and began to fall. His hands clutched at Baker's coat. But he couldn't get a grip and slid down to the floor.

Pandemonium that the judge's gavel could not control broke out in the courtroom.

"Lock the doors!" Strang shouted.

Big Dutch leaned over to say something to Matteo. "Shut up!" Matteo snapped, his dark eyes glittering in his impassive face.

The clerk looked up and smiled as Cesare appeared in the doorway. "I have the papers ready for you, Mr. Cardinali, if you'll just sign here."

Cesare took the pen from his fingers, scrawled his name on the papers and gave the pen back to the clerk. "Thank you," he said, picked up the papers and walked out.

The tight feeling was still in his chest as he stepped out into the bright sunlight. He blinked his eyes. Barbara waved to him from the car. He smiled and waved back to her, the papers in his hand flashing whitely.

Barbara smiled up at him mischievously as he crossed the curb to the car. "Congratulations, Count Cardinali."

He laughed as he walked around the car and got

into it. "You haven't read the papers, my dear. It is no longer Count Cardinali. It is just plain Mr. Cesare Cardinali."

She laughed aloud as he started the motor. "Just plain Cesare. I like that. I think it has a nice home-spun quality."

Cesare looked at her as he moved the car out into traffic. "You know, I think you're teasing me."

"No, I'm not," she said quickly. "I'm really very proud of you."

The tension was gone from his stomach now as they turned the corner away from the building. "Light a cigarette for me, will you, darling?" he asked. There was a heat growing in his loins, he could feel a pulse beating in his thighs.

She placed the cigarette between his lips. "I wonder what my mother would think," she said lightly. "Going off for a week with a man. Not married to him. Not even engaged."

He saw her smile out of the corner of his eye. "What your mother don't know won't hurt her."

Barbara was still smiling. "Of course, she might understand it if I were going with a Count. Europeans are different that way. But with just a plain mister—"

Cesare interrupted her. "You know what I think?"

She looked at him, her eyes wide. "No. What?"

The pain in his loins was growing unbearable. He reached for her hand and put it on the hard muscle of his thigh. The smile suddenly vanished from her face as she felt the tension in him. He turned his face toward her and for a moment she could see hundreds of years into his eyes. Then a veil dropped over them.

"I think your mother is a snob," he said.

STILETTO

She laughed and they fell silent as he turned the car into the Mid-Town Tunnel and the parkways to the airport. He drove by reflex, automatically, as his mind went back to Sicily, to his home. He had been there just a few weeks ago. But already it seemed as if years had passed.

What was it that Don Emilio had once called his uncle? A shylock. He laughed to himself. He wondered what Don Emilio thought of him now.

The man who lay dead behind him represented merely the principal payment on his debt. The two to come would be the interest, the accumulated interest for twelve years. Three lives for one. That should mean payment in any man's book.

He remembered how it was the night Don Emilio had presented his note.

4

The courtyard of the Castle Cardinali had been empty as Cesare pulled the car to a stop in front of the house. He turned off the motor as the door opened and an old man peeked out. When he saw Cesare his face broke into a wide happy smile. He hurried creakingly down the steps.

"Don Cesare, Don Cesare!" he cried in an ancient voice.

Cesare turned to him with a smile. "Gio!" he exclaimed.

The old man bobbed up and down before him. "You should have let us know you were coming, Don Cesare," he said. "We would have had the house ready for you."

Cesare smiled wryly. "It is an unexpected visit, Gio. I can only remain overnight. Tomorrow I must be on my way home."

A frown crossed the old man's face. "Home, Don Cesare? This is home."

Cesare started up the steps toward the house. "Yes," he said gently. "I keep forgetting. But now I live in America."

Gio pulled the valise from the back seat of the car and hurried after Cesare. "What happened in the race, Don Cesare? Did you win?"

Cesare shook his head. "No, Gio. My generator burned out. I had to stop. That is how I had time to come here."

He crossed the big chilly entrance hall and came to a stop under the portrait of his father. For a moment he stared up at the thin patrician face that looked down at him from the portrait. The war had broken him. Spiritually and physically. He had spoken out against the Germans and Il Duce ordered the lands confiscated. The old man had died soon after.

"I am sorry about your car, Don Cesare." Gio's voice came from behind him.

"The car, oh, yes." Cesare turned from the portrait and walked to the library. He hadn't been thinking about the car, not even about his father. He had just been realizing how changed it all was.

He had come back after the war and everything was gone. His uncle had come to own everything then. The bank, the lands. Everything except the castle and the title. His uncle had never forgiven his brother for legitimizing Cesare, thus depriving him of succession to the title.

No word was ever spoken aloud about it but everyone knew how the miserly little man who owned the exchange bank felt. Cesare remembered bitterly how he had gone to see his uncle.

"Signor Raimondi," he had said arrogantly, "I have been told that my father had some monies deposited with you."

Raimondi had peered at him shrewdly across the dirty black desk. "You have heard incorrectly, my nephew," he had said in his thin reedy voice. "It is, in truth, the other way round. The late Count, my good brother, unfortunately died owing me vast sums. I have here in my desk mortgages on the castle and all its lands."

It had been the truth. Everything was proper and in order. Leave it to Raimondi Cardinali to do that. For three years after the war Cesare had to live under the old man's thumb. Dependent upon him for his very existence, he came to hate him. He even had to come to his office to get money for carfare to his beloved fencing matches.

It was one such afternoon that Cesare had first met Emilio Matteo. He had been in his uncle's office in the bank when there was a great commotion outside. He turned and looked out the glass-framed door.

A handsomely dressed gray-haired man was walking toward it. There was much bowing and scraping as he walked along. "Who is that?" Cesare asked.

"Emilio Matteo," Raimondi had answered, already getting to his feet in greeting.

Cesare raised an inquiring eyebrow. He had never heard of the man.

"Matteo," his uncle explained impatiently. "One of the Dons of the Society. He has just come back from America."

Cesare smiled. The Society, they called it. The Mafia. Grown men playing like boys, spilling their blood together, calling each other Uncle and Nephew and Cousin.

"Do not smile," his uncle had snapped. "In America the Society is very important. Matteo is the richest man in all Sicily."

The door opened and Matteo came in. *"Bon giorno,* Signor Cardinali," he spoke with a heavy American accent.

"I am honored by your visit, Signor Matteo." Raimondi bowed. "How can I serve you today?"

Matteo looked inquiringly at Cesare. Raimondi hastened forward. "Allow me to present my nephew, Count Cardinali." He turned to Cesare. "Signor Matteo from America."

Matteo looked at him with a calculating eye. "Major Cardinali?"

Cesare nodded. "That was during the war."

"I have heard of you," Matteo said.

It was Cesare's turn to look at him. There were very few people that had heard of him during the war. Only those who had very special information. He wondered how much the man knew. "I am honored, sir," he said.

Raimondi wanted to get down to business. Peremptorily he dismissed Cesare. "Come back tomorrow," he said importantly, "and I will see if we can spare you the money to go to your petty fencing match."

Cesare's lips tightened, his blue eyes grew dark and cold. For a moment his body tensed. Someday the old man would go too far. Already he took upon himself too many liberties. He could feel Matteo's eyes upon him as he went to the door.

He heard Raimondi's voice as he closed it. "A fine boy but an expense. He is a relic of the past, trained for nothing, he can do no work. . . ." The door closed, shutting off the patronizing voice.

Gio had started a fire in the library and Cesare stood in front of it, holding a glass of brandy in his hand.

"I will have dinner ready in half an hour," the old man said.

Cesare nodded. He crossed the room to the desk and picked up the photograph of his mother that still stood on it. He remembered her eyes. They were blue like his own but soft and warm and kind. He remembered the day she came upon him in the garden. He was only eight years old then.

He had been absorbed watching the big green fly he had impaled on a pin in the wood struggling to get away.

"Cesare! What on earth are you doing?"

He turned and saw his mother standing there. He smiled happily and pointed. Her eyes followed his finger.

Her face had paled, then grew angry. "Cesare, stop that! Release him immediately. That's cruel."

Cesare pulled the pin from the wood but the fly still stuck to it. He looked up at his mother curiously, then down at the fly. Quickly he pulled the wings from it and dropped it on the floor and stepped on it.

His mother stared at him angrily. "Cesare, why did you do that?"

His face turned serious for a moment as he thought,

45

then it wrinkled in a winning smile. "I like to kill," he said.

His mother had stared at him for another moment, then turned and went back into the house. A year later she was dead of the fever and after that the Count took him to the castle to live and there was a succession of teachers and tutors but no one that dared speak to him with impunity.

He put the photograph down. He was getting restless. There were too many memories here. The castle reeked of the past. What he should do was sell it and become an American citizen. That was the only way to deal with the past. Cut it cleanly as if with a knife so that no trace of it remained anywhere inside you.

He thought of the message that summoned him here. The message that took him from the race, that kept him from meeting Ileana on the Riviera. He smiled to himself when he thought of Ileana. There was something about those Rumanian women, especially the demimondaines with the titles. By now she was probably on her way to California with that rich Texan.

Gio opened the library door. "Dinner is ready, Your Excellency," he said.

5

The napery was white and soft; the candles, gold and glowing; the silver, polished and gleaming. Gio had done himself proud. There was cold sliced eel, flecked with sparkling ice and hot steaming *scampi* in the warmer on the sideboard.

Gio had changed to his purple and green butler's uniform and stood proudly, holding the chair at the head of the long, white, empty table for Cesare.

Cesare sat down and reached for a napkin. "My compliments, Gio. You are indeed a genius."

Gio bobbed proudly. "I try, Your Excellency." He began to open a bottle of white Orvieto. "It is not like the old days, when the board was crowded for dinner every night. It has been a long time."

Cesare tasted the wine and nodded. It had been a long time. But the world had moved on. Time would not stand still, even for Gio. He looked down the table.

It had not been like this after the war. Then they were lucky if there was food on the table, much less cloth. He remembered the night that Matteo had come to see him. It had been the same day that he had met him in his uncle's office. He had been seated at this same table then, eating cheese and bread and apple from the naked wooden board.

There had been the sound of a car outside and Gio had gone to the door. A moment later he was back. "Signor Matteo to see Your Excellency," he had said.

Cesare told Gio to bring him in. Matteo had come into the room, his quick appraising eyes seeing everything at once. The naked board, the poor food, the steel cutlery. His face told Cesare nothing.

Cesare waved him to a seat and invited him to share the food. Matteo sat down and shook his head. He had already eaten. Cesare couldn't care less. He was of the class to whom poverty wasn't important. It was a point of annoyance, not of embarrassment. He was secure in his position.

The amenities over, Gio cleared the table and Cesare leaned back in his chair, his strong white teeth biting into the apple.

Matteo looked at him. He saw the lean rakish face, the dark, almost black, ice-blue eyes and strong jaw of the young man opposite him. He also saw the savage strength in the wrist and hands that held the apple. "Do you speak English, Major?" he asked in that language.

Cesare nodded. "I was educated in England before the war," he answered in the same language.

"Good," Matteo answered. "If you don't mind we'll speak in that language then. My Italian . . . well . . . I left here when I was a child of three."

"I don't mind," Cesare answered.

"I suppose you are wondering why I am here?" Matteo had asked.

Cesare nodded silently.

Matteo waved his hand, indicating the castle. "My father used to tell me of the wonders of the Castolo Cardinali. How they used to look up from the village and see it all gay and sparkling with light."

Cesare put the core of the apple on the table and shrugged his shoulders. "It is the fortunes of war."

Matteo answered quickly. "Or the good fortune of your uncle."

"That moneylender," Cesare said contemptuously. "He owns everything now."

Matteo looked directly into Cesare's eyes. "While he lives," he said.

"That kind is too stingy to die," Cesare said.

Matteo smiled. "In America we have a name for that kind of man. Shylock. After the usurer in the play."

Cesare smiled back. "America has a way of expressing things very pithily. Shylock. It is very good."

Matteo continued as if there hadn't been the minor diversion. "Your uncle is alone, he has no family, no other relative but you. And he has a bank with two hundred million lire."

Cesare looked at him. He recognized himself in the

older man. "I have thought about it many times. The pig does not deserve to live. But if I were to kill him it would do me no good."

Matteo shook his head seriously. "True. But if he were to die, say while you are at the fencing match one hundred fifty meters away from here, you would be a rich man again."

Cesare looked at him for a moment then got to his feet. "Gio!" he called. "Bring that bottle of Napoleon brandy. We are going into the library."

When Gio had closed the door behind him and they were alone in front of the leaping fire, Cesare turned to Matteo. "Why did you come here?" he asked directly.

Matteo smiled and picked up his brandy. "I had heard about you, Major."

"Heard what?"

"You remember of course that part of the war just before the Allies invaded Italy?" He didn't wait for Cesare to answer. "An associate of mine, who is at present in Naples, and I gave the American government a list of people to contact in preparation for that invasion. These people were members of an underground that had existed long before the war, before even the first war. The Mafioso."

Cesare didn't speak.

"I learned that you were one of the Italian officers assigned to co-operate with the O.S.S. by the Italian High Command. You were assigned to contact nine men and secure their co-operation. You murdered five of them."

"They would not co-operate," Cesare said quickly. "That was explained in my report."

Matteo smiled. "The official explanation does not concern me. I have made enough of them myself to have no faith in their veracity. But you and I know better. You see, the officials never saw the bodies of the men you killed. My friends did."

Matteo put down his glass of brandy and looked across at Cesare. "That's why I do not understand about your uncle, my friend. When death comes so joyously and easily to your hand, how you could let him live?"

Cesare looked down at him. "That was different then. It was war."

Matteo smiled. "War was only the excuse for you. There were others. The soldier down in the village when you were still a boy, the young Englishman you ran off the road in your car the last year you were in school, the German mistress of your commanding officer in Rome when she threatened to expose you to him." He looked up into Cesare's face. "You see, I have much better sources of information than the authorities."

Cesare sank into the chair opposite. He took a drink of his brandy and smiled. "So you have the information. It is of no use to you, so what can you do with it?"

Matteo shrugged his shoulders. "I don't intend to do anything with it. I have told you just to let you know that I am interested in you. You see, we can be of much mutual help to one another."

"So?"

Matteo nodded. "Circumstances have forced me to return to the land of my birth, but I am an American, not an Italian, in my heart. And also in my business interests. Unfortunately I cannot return to America for some time. Legally, that is. Of course I can go back for short periods but that is very dangerous and I cannot remain too long. Also I foresee a time when I will need an ally there, someone like yourself, someone that no one would connect me with, someone who could be of help when necessary."

Cesare stared at him. "What about your associates? Your friends in the Society? Surely you have many allies there?"

Matteo nodded. "True. But they are all known. To each other and to the police. Sooner or later there are no secrets among them."

Matteo got to his feet and walked over to the open hearth. He turned his back on the fire and looked over at Cesare. "You must be bored with the poverty of your existence by now. It is dull and drab and not at all in keeping with your nature. What would you do if you were free of all this?"

Cesare looked up. "I don't know. Travel, maybe. I would get some cars and race them. Le Mans, Turino, Sebring. There is much excitement there."

Matteo laughed. "I mean how would you make a living? Money does not last forever, you know."

Cesare shook his head. "I never thought of that. I never liked business."

Matteo took out a cigar and lit it. "Ah, the young, the thoughtless young." His voice was pleasantly tolerant. "I have an interest in an automobile company recently acquired through some legitimate associates. In several years they plan to go into the American market. If by that time you had a reputation in the racing cars, you could conceivably become the head of the American company. Would you like something like that?"

"What is there about it not to like?" Cesare answered. "But what am I expected to do in return?"

Matteo looked at him. "A favor, now and then."

"What kind of favor? I want no part of your stupid business, the petty gambling, the dope . . ."

Matteo interrupted. "Even if it should bring you undreamed-of wealth?"

Cesare laughed. "Wealth? Who needs it? All I desire is enough to do what I like to do."

Matteo laughed with him. "Good. You are not ambitious then. Another point in your favor. There is no one who need be afraid of you."

Cesare picked up his glass again. "You still have not told me what kind of favor you will ask."

Matteo stared at him. Their eyes met and locked. "Only to return the favor I will do you when your uncle dies tomorrow night while you are at the fencing match."

A long moment passed, then Cesare smiled. "Good. It is done and we are agreed."

Matteo's face was serious. "You will take the oath?"

"I will swear on it."

"Have you a knife?" Matteo asked.

A stiletto suddenly appeared in Cesare's hand. Matteo stared at it. Cesare smiled and turned it over in his hand and extended it to him, hilt forward. "This is my brother," he said. "We are always together."

Matteo took it. "Give me your hand," he said.

Cesare held out his hand. Matteo placed his left hand flat on Cesare's palm. With a quick motion he pierced each index finger with the stiletto. The blood

from each man's finger bubbled up and then ran together into their palms.

Matteo looked at him. "Our blood has mingled and
now we are of one family."

Cesare nodded.

"I will die for you," Matteo said.

"I will die for you," Cesare repeated.

Matteo released his hand and gave him back the
stiletto. He looked up into Cesare's face. He stuck his
finger into his mouth and sucked on it to stop the
bleeding. "From this time on, my nephew," he said,
"we will not meet except at my wish."

Cesare nodded. "Yes, my uncle."

"Should you find it necessary to communicate with
me, send a message to the postmaster in the village. I
will get in touch with you."

"I understand, my uncle."

That had been almost twelve years ago. True to
Matteo's word, Raimondi had died the next night
while Cesare was at the fencing match. The next five
years had gone quickly. The races and the motor cars.
The gala balls and romances. Then in 1953, just as
Emilio had said, the offer came for him to head up the
American agency of the automobile company. Much
was made of his appointment in the press. His wild
living and dangerous driving had made him an international figure of glamour. Twice he had fought duels
over women. To America he was a man from another
world.

Only once in all the twelve years had he seen Matteo.
Last year, he had gone in response to a telephone
message to a room in a boarding house over a bar in

Spanish Harlem where they had merely exchanged good wishes and Matteo had told him of his pleasure in Cesare's success. He did not stay long as a plane was waiting to take Matteo to Cuba from where he would return to Sicily. They had parted and not until a slip of paper telling him to go at once to the castle was thrust into his hand just before the start of the race did he hear from Matteo again.

The chicken cacciatore had been light and delicious, the lobster fra diavolo had been tangy and spicy and he was just putting down his napkin when a car came into the courtyard.

He could not help but watch for Gio to return from the door. A moment later Gio was back. He held an envelope in his hand.

"It was the postmaster from the village. He said he had this special letter to deliver to you."

Cesare took it from him and ripped it open. It was two pages of closely typewritten instructions. He read it quickly, then read it again. Slowly he put the letter down on the table and reached for the espresso.

Twelve years had passed. And Don Emilio had presented his note for payment. With interest.

6

Las Vegas is a night town. Outside the hotels are the pools, clear, filtered and aquamarine, but no one sits around them except the tourists and the hustlers who work the hotels and keep their tans as a kind of pancake makeup of their trade. Inside the lobbies it is always night.

Someone once said never let them see the daylight. There is something about the harsh white light of day that interferes with the gambler's sense of reality. The reality of the spinning roulette wheel, the dull thumping of dice on hard felt-covered tables, the reality of the fever to win, the reality of the shifting desert sands on which the town was built.

Here is the prize, the great adventure, the promise of all the tomorrows. Free money. And everything else runs second to it. Sex, business, laughter. Free money. Pull the handle on the slot machines. It may be your turn at the jackpot.

They came out of the dining-room-theater, still laughing at the comedy of one of the world's greatest entertainers. They paused, looking down into the lobby of the gambling casino.

It was ten o'clock at night and the tables at the Maharajah were crowded with the people who had come from the dinner show. Cesare's eyes searched the room.

"You didn't hear what I asked," Barbara said.

Cesare turned and looked down at her. His eyes were glowing with a strange excitement. "No, I didn't, my dear. What was it?"

Barbara looked up at him. Another man would have apologized or protested that he had heard. He merely said that he hadn't. "Dice or roulette, I asked."

He smiled suddenly. "Roulette. I have given enough to those crazy little cubes of ivory. I will never understand them."

They began to walk down toward the roulette tables. "Too bad they don't play baccarat here. Now there is a game for the civilized human being. For that some skill is needed, merely having luck is not enough."

Barbara turned toward a table. He held her arm. "Not this one. It is too crowded. Over here."

It was the table opposite the one she had been going to but he had been right: it was less crowded. He pulled out a stool for her and she sat down. She smiled up at him. "Feel lucky tonight?"

He nodded his head and smiled back at her. "Very lucky," he said, placing a pile of chips in front of her.

STILETTO

In New York the telephone on Baker's desk began to ring. He put down the container of coffee and picked it up.

"Jordan calling from Las Vegas," the operator said.

"Put him on," he answered.

Ted Jordan came on the wire. "Hello, George, how we doin'?"

"No good," Baker answered wearily. "We're up the creek. We still can't figure out how Dinty Adams was killed. How's your boy holding up?"

Jordan laughed. "Just great. Right now he's out at the roulette wheel betting like there's no tomorrow."

"Is he covered?" Baker asked anxiously.

"I got a man on each side of him and one standing right behind him. Nobody can get anywhere near him."

"I'm still nervous. We thought we had Adams covered too and look what happened."

"If you're that worried, George," Jordan said, "why don't we just lock him up. We can keep him away from everybody in there."

"You know the deal," Baker replied. "If we do that, the defense will know who the witnesses are before we get them into court. And if they know, the witnesses won't talk and there goes our case."

"Matteo must be laughing like hell right this minute," Jordan said.

"He won't when we get back into court," Baker promised.

"My boy is giving twenty to one that he never gets into that courtroom," Jordan said.

Baker's voice was incredulous. "You mean to say he

really believes that he'll be killed? And he's still going out to the casinos?"

"Yeah," Jordan answered laconically. "He says there's nothing anybody can do about it so he might as well live it up while he can."

Baker put down the telephone and picked up the container of coffee again. There was the one thing he could never understand about them. They were cowards, pimps and murderers but there was still something in them that gave them a fatalistic approach to life. Or was it death? He just didn't know.

The Twister sat at the roulette table, his gaze concentrated on the wheel. It stopped and the ball bounced into the red twenty. He made another note on the small sheet of paper. Quickly he added up the columns. He was right. The wheel was running toward the black tonight. Time for him to make his move. He pushed a small pile of chips onto the black.

He heard Jordan come up behind him. He didn't turn around. The bodyguard behind him spoke. "Could you spell me for a few minutes, Ted? I gotta get to the john before I bust."

He didn't hear Jordan's reply. The ball bounced into the red. He lost. He looked down and pushed another pile of chips on the black.

Cesare turned around and looked at the Twister while Barbara concentrated on the spinning wheel. Matteo's note had been very specific. For almost three days now, Cesare had been watching the Twister.

The bodyguards were there. They were always there. One on each side of him and one standing back to back with him, his eyes constantly alert. Now the last one went away but another took his place. Cesare turned away just as the man's gaze began to sweep toward him. He had seen enough. With a little bit of luck— He smiled to himself as the phrase jumped through his mind. Everybody used it out here. With a little bit of luck he would complete his business here tonight.

He tapped Barbara on the shoulder. "I'll get you a drink," he said.

She looked up at him and smiled and then turned back, absorbed in the game. He began to walk toward the lounge. He walked around the Twister's table and glanced back.

He could see the Twister's face now, a look of concentration on it. Opposite the Twister sat a big blond girl. Cesare stared for a moment. The girl leaned forward and he could see her full breasts pull against the two thin straps that held up her dress. Suddenly he began to smile. He knew how he would do it now. It was all because of a joke. A very old joke that was told to everyone who came to Las Vegas.

Jordan looked around him wearily. He wished the job was over. When he came to the F.B.I. fresh from law school and filled with the propaganda, he envisioned an exciting life filled with chasing criminals and spies. He never thought he would spend three months playing chief nursemaid to a cheap hood.

He looked at the table opposite him. That couple was there again. A good-looking couple. He remembered noticing them the first night. There was something familiar about them. As if he had seen them before. With his usual thoroughness he had checked on them.

The girl was one of the best-known models in America. Barbara Lang, the "Smoke and Flame" girl whose face he had seen in a thousand cosmetic ads and the man was Cesare Cardinali. Count Cardinali, the society racing-car driver.

He saw Cesare say something to the girl and begin to walk away. Some of the things he had read about the man came to mind. There was a guy who really lived. Leave it to those rich Europeans. They didn't give a damn for anybody. They had a ball everywhere they went. Here he was with one of the most beautiful dames in America and just as cool as you could be. He looked at the girl again. All the promise the advertisements held was right there. Some guys had all the luck.

Cesare waited until the blonde sat up straight on her stool. Petulantly she turned to her escort, a fat little man. He gave her some bills from a big roll and she turned back to the table. Cesare started down from the lounge, holding a drink in his left hand.

He walked down the aisle behind the blonde and hesitated for a moment. The croupier turned the wheel and dropped the ball. Cesare's hand moved quickly behind the blonde's back and he started to walk around the table toward his own.

He could feel the throbbing begin in his temples and the pain. It was always like this. The pain would start there, and then, step by step, move down into his body. He knew the pain now and had a long time ago ceased to fear it. It was the pain of excitement, of danger, of looking into the abyss of time, the hell of oblivion.

He was behind the Twister who was resting his chin in his hands, supported by his elbows on the table edge. The bodyguard was just starting to turn toward him when the scream came.

The bodyguard whirled, his hand streaking toward his shoulder holster. Cesare moved quickly. Across the table, the blonde fought to hold her dress over her bosom. It was a losing battle. There was too much of her.

Cesare let go of the stiletto and felt the knife spring back into his sleeve. The Twister still sat quietly on his stool, not moving. The bodyguard turned back. Cesare could see him smiling as Barbara took her drink.

The blonde was passing their table now, the fat little man hurrying after her. Her high-pitched voice floated back to them. "They didn't break I tell you, they didn't! They were cut! Somebody—"

"Ssh! Please, baby! Everybody's looking!" the little man pleaded.

"I don't give a damn!" the blonde retorted as they hurried up the steps toward the lounge.

Cesare and Barbara laughed and she turned back to the table to make another bet.

Jordan turned around and looked down at the Twister. He was sitting there not moving, his chin in his hands. The wheel stopped. It was on the black. The croupier pushed a pile of chips to join the others on the table. The Twister didn't move.

The wheel started to spin again. Jordan looked at one of the other bodyguards. The man shrugged his shoulders.

"Get your bets down, ladies and gentlemen," the croupier called in his soft monotone. A few more bets came down and the croupier threw the ball into the wheel. The pile in front of the Twister grew. It was black again. He didn't move.

The pain bound Cesare's chest now, making it difficult for him to breathe. He looked down at Barbara. "This is no way to spend our last night in Las Vegas," he said. "In this crowded place with all these stupid people."

She looked up at him. A faint smile lurked in the corners of her mouth. "Just what do you have in mind?" she asked.

Cesare forced himself to smile. "Just the two of us. Alone."

Excitement began to grow in her eyes. She could feel the current flowing out of him but couldn't resist a tease. "It was the blonde that did it. There was too much for any man."

"That's not true," he answered quickly. He reached for her hand.

His palm was warm and moist as if he had a fever. She looked up at him quickly. "Are you all right?"

"I'm fine," he answered. "I'm just bored with this, bored with all these people who think of nothing but money. I want to be with you. I want to feel the life inside you."

Her lips were suddenly dry. She could feel a heat suddenly surging inside her. Inside her mind there was a flashing image of his muscular thrusting body. She held his hand tightly and looked up into his face.

There was an intensity that had not been there a

moment before. "We'll have cold champagne for before," he said. "And warm brandy for after."

She moved off the seat as if in a haze. Her legs felt curiously weak. She tried to smile up at him. "And then cold champagne again?" she whispered.

Jordan looked down at the Twister. This was the fourth time that black had won. The chips in front of the Twister amounted to almost nine thousand dollars now. "Don't press your luck, Jake. Better pick up some of that loot." He smiled, tapping the witness on the shoulder.

Grotesquely the witness slid forward, face down on the table, his hands knocking the chips away from him, his face coming to rest on a pile of them.

A woman screamed. Jordan lifted the Twister's head. His eyes were open, expressionless. Jordan dropped his hand. "Help me get him out of here!" he snapped.

The bodyguards moved quickly. They lifted the Twister expertly and started toward the assistant manager's office. There was a brief moment of hysteria. But only a moment.

The calm monotonous voices of the house men spoke up, quietly reassuring. "It's all right, folks. The man just fainted. It's all right."

Such is the promise of Las Vegas—the free money, the dream of tomorrow—that in a moment the wheel began to turn again and the man was all but forgotten by those who had sat at the table with him.

That is by all but the croupier who was fired the next morning for stealing five thousand dollars from the pile of chips that had lain in front of the Twister.

They turned to look as the men hurried past them carrying the Twister. Barbara looked up into Cesare's face.

His eyes were cold and shining, his mouth was slightly open as if in a twisted smile. He turned to look after them then back to her.

A shiver ran through her. "Why do you look like that?"

His face softened suddenly and his lips turned to a real smile. "I was just thinking that they have everything figured here. No matter what you do you can't win."

He took a deep breath. The pain was in his gut now. He could hardly keep from crying out with it. "Come," he said. "There is nothing for us here."

The telephone on Baker's desk began to ring again just as he started to leave the office. He walked back and picked it up.

It was Jordan. His voice crackled excitedly through the telephone. "They just killed the Twister!"

Slowly Baker sank into his seat. "Killed? How?"

"Stiletto! The same way they got Adams." Jordan's voice almost broke. "I'm sorry, George. We were on him every minute. I don't know how they did it. There were over a thousand people in that casino tonight."

Baker's mind suddenly cleared. "Look," he said. "Call me back in an hour. I want to call Miami and make sure that Vanicola is okay."

He pressed down the button on the phone then let it come up again. The operator came on. "Get me Special Agent Stanley in Miami Beach," he said.

STILETTO

They know the witnesses, he thought to himself while the call was going through. They know. All the secrecy, all the preparation would be for nothing.

They know.

7

The room was silent except for the soft whisper of her sleep. He stared up at the ceiling, his eyes wide. It was so many years ago he had almost forgotten.

The war. There had been nothing like it since. Everything else was a substitute. A substitute for death. The great danger, the great excitement, the feeling of power that ran through your body with the knowledge of the death-force inside you tearing its way out, bringing you closer to your own destiny.

He smiled slowly into the dark, a feeling of well-being permeating his body. He reached for a cigarette on the night table. The package was empty.

He slid silently out of the bed and crossed the room to the dresser, took a cigarette from the package there and lit it. Through the terrace doors the first gray streaks of dawn were lifting the horizon.

"Cesare." Her voice was a whisper from the bed.

He turned toward her. He could not see her in the dark. "Yes?"

"Open the second bottle of champagne." Her voice was husky with sleep.

"We already did," he said.

"But I'm still thirsty," she said in a small girl's voice.

Cesare laughed almost inaudibly. "You are an insatiable woman."

He heard the rustle of the sheets as she sat up. "I can't help it if I'm still thirsty, can I?"

He laughed again. "I guess you can't," he answered and went out onto the terrace.

The night was still and in the distance he could hear the sound of the crickets and the faint dry whisper of the desert wind. The dark blue of the sky was lightening with the thrust of morning. He leaned against the railing looking out into the desert.

She came out onto the terrace behind him. He didn't turn around. She came up close behind him and slipped her arms around his chest and leaned her head against his naked back.

"It will soon be morning," she said.

"I know," he answered.

She pressed her lips to his shoulder. "Your skin is smooth and clean and soft. Sometimes I wonder where all the fierce driving strength comes from. I didn't know a man could be like you."

He laughed, turning around. "It must be the wines I drank when I was a boy. The wines of Sicily are supposed to be good for your blood and your skin."

She looked up into his face. There were some things

about him she would never understand. "When you make love to me, why do you always say you are dying?" she asked in a wondering tone. "What a strange thing to say at a time like that."

He smiled down at her. "That is what we Italians call it. The little death."

"Why?" she asked. "When everything inside you is bursting open and being born, why should you say it is like dying?"

The smile faded from his lips. "Is it not? Is not each birth the beginning of death? Do you not feel the pain of it?"

She shook her head. "No. Only the lifting joy of it." She looked up into his eyes. "Maybe that's the difference between us. Maybe that's why I feel even when you're closest to me that there's a part of you that's far away in a world I know nothing about."

"That's silly," he said.

"No, it's not," she said quickly. "Like the way you looked when they carried that man past us. One moment it was like I could feel you inside me, right in that room with all those people. The next moment they came by and you were gone. He was dead, wasn't he?"

He stared down at her. "What makes you say that?"

"He was dead," she whispered. "I could tell from the expression on your face. You knew. Nobody else knew. But you knew."

"That's a foolish thing to say," he said lightly. "How would I know?"

She shook her head. "I don't know. But it was the same expression you had on your face when you came out of the building the day we started on our trip.

71

Then when we opened the newspapers on the plane we read about that man being killed in the court around the corner from where we were."

She placed her head against his chest and did not see the slowly tightening expression of his face. "I don't have to read tomorrow's papers to know that the man downstairs was killed. I can feel it. I wonder what it will be like in Miami?"

He wondered if she could feel his heart beginning to thump through his naked flesh. He forced his voice to be light. "Like it always is. Sunny and warm."

She looked up into his eyes. "That's not what I meant, darling. I mean will someone die there too?"

The veil was gone from his eyes and she was looking deep into them. "People die everywhere, everyday," he said.

She felt almost hypnotized. "You're not the Angel of Death, are you, darling?"

He laughed suddenly and the veil was back. "Now that is a crazy thing to say."

"It's not really," she spoke slowly. "I read in a story once about a girl who fell in love with the Angel of Death."

His hand caught the back of her head and held her close to his chest. "What happened to her?" he asked.

He could feel her lips move against his breast. "She died. When he knew that she knew who he was, he had to take her with him."

She looked up at him suddenly. "Will you take me with you, Cesare?"

His hand tightened in the long hair that hung down her shoulders, pulling her head back so that her face turned up toward him. "I will take you with me," he said, placing his mouth brutally on her lips.

He could hear her gasp of pain as his free hand took her breast. She turned her face from him and cried aloud, "Cesare! You're hurting me!"

He ground her face to his naked chest and moved her head slowly in a widening circle, never stopping the pressure of his hand on her breast. He heard her moan softly and a torrent began to rise inside him. The circle became wider, she was moaning steadily now as she sank slowly to her knees.

She cried aloud at his growing strength. "Cesare! Stop, please stop! The pain, I can't stand the pain!"

He was smiling now. There was power inside him. And life. And death. His voice seemed to come from some distant place outside him. "It is time you learned, my dear, how exquisite the pleasure of pain can be."

"Don't, Cesare, don't!" Her body began to shiver in a wild convulsion. "I can't stand the pain! I am dying!"

He looked down at her and let go suddenly. She almost fell, then her hands caught his hips and she clung to him, sobbing, "Cesare, I love you! I love you!"

8

Miami Beach is a sun town built on a sterile strip of sand along the Florida coast. Each year by an artificial insemination of capital it gives birth to a new hotel. The St. Tropez is this year's new hotel.

Not far from the Fontainebleu and Eden Roc, the St. Tropez rises eleven stories into the ocean sky in an architectural style vaguely reminiscent of a Picasso impression of the palace at Monte Carlo. The Floridians, who judge beauty by the amount of rental per room in season, call it the most beautiful hotel ever built. The rental per room is eighty dollars a day.

It has a ten-foot-wide beach fronting on the ocean on which no one is ever seen except the tourists in off season. It also has a cloverleaf pool that has been proclaimed as the largest pool ever built. It is completely surrounded by four tiers of cabanas, stepped back so they resemble bleachers in a ball park and do not obstruct the sun. Each cabana is complete with private bath and telephone, card table, chairs and small refrigerator.

By three o'clock in the afternoon each cabana has a gin game going full blast, the players generally sitting in their shorts and swim suits, shielded from the sun they waste at the going rate per diem. Around the pool on long wooden lounge chairs are the sun worshipers, their bodies glistening with oil and lotions, trying to make the most of their already overburdened pocketbooks.

Sam Vanicola was standing at the window of the suite in the St. Tropez, looking down at the pool. He was a big man. Even when he was a punk kid running errands for Lepke in Brooklyn, he was big. He weighed over two hundred pounds then, now he weighed two-forty on his five-eleven frame.

He gave a snort of disgust and came back into the room where three men were playing cards. He looked down at them. "This is a lot of crap!" he announced.

Special Agent Stanley looked up at him. "We got our orders, Sam," he said genially.

"Orders, borders!" Vanicola snorted. "Look, it didn't mean nuttin' when they kept Abe Reles locked up in his hotel room in the Half Moon in Brooklyn. They got to him anyway."

Stanley smiled again. "How do you know, Sam? He went out the window and they said it was suicide."

"That's a horse laugh!" Vanicola replied. "I knew him. That boy was pushed. He'd never jump."

"Besides," Stanley persisted. "That was twenty years ago. Things are different now."

Vanicola laughed. "They sure are," he said derisively. "Dinky Adams gets his on his way into court, Jake the Twister in a room with a thousand people—and you tell me things are different."

Stanley fell silent. He exchanged glances with the other agents. They didn't speak.

Vanicola took a cigar out of his pocket, walked across the room and sat down on the couch. He bit the end off the cigar and spat it out on the rug. He lit it and leaned back, looking at them. His voice was less harsh now. "Now look, you guys. I'm a taxpayer too. The guvviment is spending two C's a day of my good money to keep me in a joint like this. What for they spending the dough if nobody gets any benefit out of it?"

Stanley got up from his chair. "You'd rather sit in the pokey?" he asked.

Vanicola stared up at him. "Don't make me laugh, Stanley. You do and I clam up. You ain't got no more chances left after me."

"What's the matter with you anyway, Sam?" Stanley cried out in sheer frustration. "What've you got against staying alive?"

Vanicola's eyes were suddenly serious. "The way I look at it I was dead the day you picked me up. If I didn't talk you had me on a murder rap; if I did, it would only be a question of time before the boys got to me. Now I'm runnin' out of time real fast. So why don't you call up your boss and tell him all I wanna do is spend an hour or two down at that pool every afternoon? I'll go along with everything else you say."

Stanley walked over to the window and looked down

at the pool. There was the usual number of people down there. Vanicola's voice came from the couch.

"Nobody can get to me down there. You can cover every entrance. There are only two."

Stanley turned and went into the next room and closed the door behind him. Vanicola looked over at the two agents seated at the card table. They began to play gin again. He sat there silently, puffing at his cigar.

A few minutes later Stanley came out. He crossed the room and stood in front of Vanicola. "Okay, Sam, you get what you want. But, remember, if you see anything we don't, recognize anyone, you let us know right away. We don't want anything to happen to you."

Vanicola got out of the chair and walked over to the window. He looked down at the pool. "Sure, sure," he agreed quickly. "I ain't that much in a hurry to croak."

Stanley walked back to the card table and sat down. Vanicola turned and looked after him. He smiled but there was no humor in his eyes. "At least I'll be sure of one thing," Vanicola said.

One of the agents looked up at him. "What's that, Sam?"

"Getting a pretty good tan," he answered. "Ain't nobody who'll come to see me when they lay me out won't be able to tell where I spent the winter."

Barbara was standing on the balcony looking out at the ocean when she heard the telephone ringing in the room. She walked inside and picked it up.

"New York calling Count Cardinali," the operator said.

She covered the mouthpiece with her hand. "Cesare, there's a call for you," she called into the bedroom.

He came into the room in his swimming shorts, the deep tan he had already acquired in the few days they had been here contrasting with the white trunks. He took the telephone from her hand. "Cardinali speaking," he said into it.

The operator's voice crackled through the receiver. "All right," Cesare said. "Put her on." He looked across at Barbara. "It's Miss Martin, my secretary."

Barbara nodded and went outside on the balcony again. She could hear faint snatches of his conversation. It had something to do with a car that was in Palm Beach. After a few minutes he put down the telephone. He didn't come out. When she turned around, he was seated at the desk making a few notes on a scratch pad. She went back inside.

He looked up at her and smiled. "Forgive me," he said. "Business."

She looked down at him and nodded slowly. This was the last day of the week they had planned together. "I wish the week were only beginning," she said.

"So do I," he answered.

"I hate to think that tomorrow we'll be back in New York and it will be cold and bleak and we won't be warm like this until summer. I wish we could stay here forever."

He smiled. "That is always the trouble. Holidays must have an end."

"Must ours?" she asked, not speaking of the holiday at all.

He knew what she meant. "It must," he said quietly.

"I have my business to go back to. You have your work."

A kind of sadness was in her. She knew now that the only one she had been fooling when she agreed to start this week was herself. What had happened between them was no more than a holiday for him. "Does anybody really know you, Cesare?"

A look of surprise leaped into his eyes. "That's a funny question," he answered.

Suddenly she wanted to touch him, to make him feel her reality. She turned away so that her hands would not reach for him. "No, it's not," she said. "Most people think you're a playboy. I know you're not."

Cesare walked around the desk to her. "I have been very fortunate. It is good for my business to do what I like to do."

She looked up into his eyes. "Is that the reason for the girls like me? To build your reputation along with the fast cars? Because it's good for your business?"

He took her hand. "There are no girls like you."

"No?" she said, getting angry with herself for not being able to stop. "What about that Baroness? De Bronczki or something? A month ago the papers were full of how you were chasing her all over Europe."

"Ileana?" He chuckled. "I've known her since she was a child. Our families were old friends. Besides she doesn't matter now. She's in California with a rich Texan. She has a taste for rich Texans."

Her eyes fell. "I'm sorry," she said.

He put his hand under her chin and lifted her face up. "I have an idea," he said. "There is a car my office wants me to look at in Palm Beach. Instead of flying back to New York tonight, let's pick up the car and drive back. I am bored with planes anyway and that way we can stretch our holiday."

She began to smile. Maybe she had been wrong about him. Maybe it was not just a holiday. "That will be wonderful!"

He looked down at his wristwatch. "It's almost three o'clock," he said. "We have time for one more swim. We can have dinner in Palm Beach and be in Jacksonville before morning."

Vanicola came out of the cabana bathroom. He had on his swimming trunks, of a bright Hawaiian pattern. He stood in the shadows of the cabana and looked down at the F.B.I. men. "Okay if I get my ration of sunshine now?"

The agents exchanged glances and Stanley turned and checked the men at the exits. They caught his look and nodded. He got to his feet. "I guess it's okay," he said grudgingly.

The other two agents got to their feet. Vanicola started down toward the pool, picking his way carefully around the sunbathers stretched out on the lounge chairs. They stood around him as he took a plastic float from the rack and slid it into the water. He walked down the steps into the pool and clumsily stretched on the float.

Stanley was studying the people around them. The youngest agent looked at him. "See anything, chief?"

Stanley shook his head. "No. I guess it's safe enough. They aren't wearing enough clothes around here to conceal any weapons."

The young man grinned, his eyes going over some of the girls lounging at poolside. "Some of those babes aren't wearing enough to conceal their weapons either."

Stanley didn't smile. Nothing was funny to him right now.

Vanicola spoke to them from the pool where he was stretched on his back on the raft. "I told you guys there was nothing to worry about." He grinned. "This is the third day we been out and nothing's happened yet. Let me know when ten minutes are up and I'll turn over. I don't want to get fried."

"Okay," Stanley answered. He sat down on a chair near poolside. He would be glad when this job was over.

Vanicola floated away. As the agents idly watched the swimmers, their tension gradually began to ease off.

Cesare saw them from across the pool. He glanced at Barbara. She was lying on her stomach, her back to the sun, her eyes closed. He could feel his heart begin to pound. He looked across the pool again.

Vanicola was floating out toward the center of the cloverleaf where a group of youngsters were frolicking. Their voices came back to Cesare. Unconsciously his hand dropped to his waist. He could feel the stiletto in the concealed sheath beneath his trunks. He took his hand away quickly.

One of the bodyguards was getting up now. He called something to Vanicola. Vanicola sat up clumsily and almost fell into the water, then he turned around and stretched out face down on the float. The bodyguard sat down again.

STILETTO

Cesare glanced at Barbara. She was still lying quietly. He rose swiftly, took a deep breath and dove into the water. He went down deep, his eyes straining as he swam out to the center of the pool.

Barbara sat up when she heard the splash of his dive. "Cesare," she called.

But he was already gone, bubbles trailing in his wake. She blinked her eyes and smiled. In some ways he was like a small boy. For three days now he had been practicing swimming underwater across the pool and back. She glanced up at the clock on the cabana wall. It was twenty minutes to four. She began to gather up her things. It was getting late and they would have to leave soon.

She had just finished retouching her lipstick when his head came up over the edge of the pool near her. His mouth was open in a strange grin as he gulped air into his lungs. He stared at her as if she were far away.

"Did you make it this time?" she asked, smiling.

"I made it," he answered as he pulled himself out of the pool.

Her voice was shocked. "Cesare!"

A flash of fear leaped into his eyes. His hand felt for the stiletto. It was there, back in the sheath. He looked at her, then followed her gaze back down to himself. He caught the robe she flung at him and wrapped it around himself. She was laughing now as he walked toward her. "Cesare, you are like a little boy. The minute you get excited, it shows," she teased.

He grinned at her without embarrassment. He took her hand and pulled her to her feet. "Didn't I tell you that we Sicilians are very basic people?" He laughed.

She picked up her beach bag and, still laughing, they walked back into the hotel.

The telephone in the cabana began to ring. Stanley got to his feet. "Keep an eye on him while I get the phone," he said to the other agents.

They nodded and he walked back into the cabana. The youngest agent looked around and then spoke to the other man. "I'd like to come back here sometime when I'm not working."

The other man grinned. "You couldn't afford it. Everything comes high in this place."

Stanley came back. For the first time in several days, he was smiling. "Come on," he said to them. "Let's get him out of there. We're going to New York tonight."

The other men got to their feet and they all turned toward the pool. Stanley's voice carried over to the raft. "Okay, Sam. Come on in. Your ten minutes are up."

But more than ten minutes were up for Sam. Sam Vanicola was lying there dead on the slowly sinking raft, his face pressed close to the plexiglass shield, looking into the water. And even the last memory was gone from his mind now. The sight of Cesare's grinning face coming up at him from the bottom of the pool just before his heart exploded in a pain he never knew he could feel.

9

The Sunshine State Parkway runs north from Miami to Fort Pierce, past the swamps and marshes and citrus groves that dot the Florida Atlantic Coast. And many times at night in the early winter the fog rolls in from the suddenly cooling seas and, mixed with the smoke from the smudge pots, forms a shroudlike mist that clings to the roadway like a down quilt on a feather bed.

The powerful engine in the Ghia convertible throbbed as Barbara reached over and turned on the radio. The music filled the car and she peered over the wheel, the powerful headlights biting through the first mist. "The fog's coming in," she said.

Cesare nodded. "Want me to put the top up?" he asked.

"Let it go for a while," she answered. "I'm comfortable."

They drove along in silence for a few minutes then the announcer's voice broke into the music. "And now, the eleven o'clock news from Miami."

Cesare looked at her. She was driving with a fierce concentration on the road before her. The newscaster came on.

"With the murder of Sam Vanicola in the swimming pool of the St. Tropez Hotel here in Miami Beach this afternoon, the government announced tonight in New York the complete collapse of its case against the four alleged leaders of the Syndicate. It was disclosed also that the murder weapon used in each case was a stiletto. The stiletto is a weapon of vengeance that originated in Italy about the time of the Borgias. It was a great favorite of assassins of that period due to the fact that its peculiar shape caused internal hemorrhaging while the surface wound itself closed after the weapon was withdrawn from the victim. The police and the F.B.I. attach a great deal of significance to this fact and are pressing every means at their disposal to discover clues that would lead them to the identity of the killer or killers. Meanwhile in Washington—"

Cesare reached over and turned off the radio. "News is so dull these days," he said with a short laugh. "Murder and crime all the time. Can't they find anything else to talk about?"

Barbara didn't answer. Her eyes seemed fastened to the road.

He laughed again. "Wake up, sleepy one. You're driving."

"I'm awake," she said.

"That's good to know." He smiled. "I feel better."

Her voice was thoughtful. "I was just thinking."

"About what?" he asked.

"About the man that died in the pool. I wonder which one he was. If I saw him or he saw me."

"That's a strange thought," he said. "Why do you think it?"

Her eyes still were on the road. "Maybe if we had spoken to each other I might have warned him. I don't know."

He laughed shortly. "What would you have warned him about? You did not know what was to happen."

She glanced at him. Her eyes were deep and troubled. "I could have told him about the Angel of Death. And how it followed us from New York to Las Vegas and then to Miami." She shivered slightly. "Do you think he is still following us, Cesare?"

"Now you are being silly," he said. "You better pull over here and let me drive. You're letting all this nonsense upset you."

Silently she put on the right turn indicator and began to slow up. She pulled the car off on a shoulder of the road and came to a stop. She turned to look at him.

"It is just as well," he said. "I know the road up ahead. There is a very narrow bridge and the fog is beginning to thicken."

"I'm not arguing," she said. "You drive. But be careful."

"I'll be careful." He laughed and pulled her to him. He kissed her.

Her lips were cold and they clung to his mouth. "I don't care if you are the Angel of Death," she whispered. "Being with you has made me happier than I've ever been in my whole life."

He couldn't suppress the question that rose to his lips. "What would you do if I were?"

She looked up at him questioningly. "Now *you're* being silly," she said.

Something inside was driving him on. Maybe if she knew, if she could understand, it wouldn't all seem so empty. Why did he have to be the only one that felt as he did? "I could have been the killer," he said slowly. "After all we were each place where a murder happened."

She stared up at him, then she began to smile. "So were hundreds of others. Sometimes, Cesare, I think that you're as crazy as I am."

He laughed and got out of the car. He walked around to her side of the car and looked down at her. She had taken out her lipstick and was beginning to apply it.

"Be a dear, will you, and give me some light?" she said without looking up. "I'm afraid I'll make a mess of this."

He flicked on his lighter and looked down at her. He could feel his lips tightening across his teeth.

She looked up at him. "What are you staring at?" she asked curiously.

"You," he answered tightly. "You're very beautiful."

She smiled. "That deserves another kiss before I put the lipstick on."

He bent over the side of the car and kissed her. Her lips were warmer now, they moved against his. "Cesare," she whispered. "I'm afraid I'm beginning to love you so very much that it doesn't really matter any more whether you killed those men or not."

He straightened up and she turned to begin to apply

the lipstick again. He looked down. There was the white flesh of her neck, just below where the short curls turned into ringlets. He raised his right hand, palm out and flat. There was nothing else he could do. Already she had put too many facts together. Death led to death and murder was like concentric ripples in a pool that spread out and out until they reached farther and farther away from the victim and the violator. He brought his hand down sharply in a vicious judo chop.

The lipstick shot from her hand like a bullet and smashed into the dashboard and then fell tinkling to the floor of the car. He stared down at her, his heart bursting inside him.

She lay slumped across the wheel, one hand still closed on it, her head in an odd position. He was glad he could not see her eyes. He looked around quickly. There were no cars coming. He ran around to the other side of the car and got into it on the seat beside her. He reached over and turned the key, starting the motor. It caught with a roar.

He looked around again. The road was still empty. He reached into his sleeve and took out the stiletto and the hook spring to which it was attached. With a quick motion of his hand he flung it far into the darkness and heard it sink into the watery marsh on the other side of the shoulder. He put the car into gear and, steering from his side, moved it out into the road.

He jammed his foot down on the accelerator. The bridge should be less than a mile from here. In a moment the car was doing eighty. He peered through the fog. Barbara slumped toward him.

There was the bridge. With a muttered curse, he

shoved her back under the wheel. He took his foot from the accelerator and pulled both feet up under him. He held the wheel steady, driving the car right at the concrete abutment at the side of the bridge.

He sprang high into the air in an arcing dive at almost the moment of impact. The speed of the car pushed him forward and he tumbled awkwardly through the air toward the water.

The sound of the crash came to his ears at almost the same moment he hit the water. It was cold and black and murky and he gasped for breath. He was going down and down, his lungs were bursting, he would never come up. Frantically his arms flailed the water. The reeds clung to him, trying to keep him down. Then he saw the sky above him again.

He pulled himself toward the shore. There was a pain inside him now, racing all through his body. He felt his feet touch the land and stumbled to his knees. He crawled out of the water slowly and then sprawled out on the ground. His mouth felt filled with dirt and his face scratched and burning.

The ground was moist and clammy and its chill raced through him. He began to shudder convulsively, digging his fingers into the earth, clinging to it. Then he closed his eyes and the night came up and over him.

Baker leaned back in his chair and stared out the window. The white winter sun formed sharp patterns on the buildings. Three days had passed since Vanicola had died and they were exactly nowhere. He looked down the desk at the men seated opposite. There was Captain Strang of the New York Police, Jordan in from Las Vegas and Stanley up from Miami.

He spread his hands on the desk in a gesture of defeat. "That's the story. I'm not blaming any one of you, the responsibility was mine and I accept it. Tomorrow morning I'm due in Washington to see the chief. Senator Bratton is on the Bureau's back and the chief wants a personal report."

"What are you going to tell him, George?" Stanley asked.

"What can I tell him?" Baker answered rhetorically. "I don't know any more than he does." He picked up an envelope from the desk. "My resignation's in here. I'm turning it in tomorrow."

"Wait a minute," Jordan said. "The chief hasn't asked for your scalp."

Baker smiled wryly. "Come on, Ted, don't be naïve. You know the chief as well as I do. He doesn't like failure."

As they fell silent Baker absently pressed the button on the slide projector on his desk. It jumped to life and threw a picture on the wall. It was a scene of the crowd inside the corridor of the courthouse.

"What've you got there?" Jordan asked.

Baker pressed the button idly. "Pictures of the corridor taken by newspaper photographers as Dinky Adams was going into the courtroom." He pressed another button and the scene changed. "I've looked at them a thousand times. You'd think with all the pictures they took, we'd find something. Not one of them took the picture at the time we needed it."

He hit the button and the scene changed again. "I forgot you fellows didn't see it yet."

He stared for a moment then pressed the button again.

"Wait a minute," Stanley said, an excitement rising in his voice. "Can you go back to the picture you had on before this one?"

Baker hit the button. Stanley got up and walked over to the wall and looked closely at the picture. He put a finger out and pointed to a man. "Have you got a doohickey on that machine that will enlarge the picture of this guy in the green alpine hat?"

Baker laughed disgustedly. Another blank. "That hat isn't green. It's the wall paint."

Captain Strang interrupted. "It was green, George. I remember noticing it in the crowd."

Swiftly Baker fiddled with the lens. Now there was only one man's face on the screen. There was only a side angle of the face but there was no mistaking the hat.

"I've seen that hat before," Stanley said.

"There are lots of hats like that," Baker said.

"But not faces like that," Jordan said suddenly. "I know that one."

They turned to him. "That's Count Cardinali," he said. "The racing-car driver. He was at the table next to us in Vegas. He was there with the girl who models for all those 'Smoke and Flame' cosmetic ads, Barbara Lang."

Stanley jumped to his feet, almost sputtering. "They were at the St. Tropez too. That's where I saw the hat. I was in the lobby when they checked in and he was wearing it!"

Baker stared at them. Maybe it wasn't over yet. He picked up the telephone and spoke into it. "I want a complete I.D. file on Count Cardinali. The works, from the day he was born until yesterday!"

92

STILETTO

He put down the telephone, still looking at them. "Do you have any idea where he may be right now?"

"I do," Captain Strang answered. He took a newspaper out of his pocket and opened it on the desk. He pointed to the top corner of the page.

Baker looked down at it. There was a picture of Cardinali over the story. The headline read, *Famous Sportsman Out of Hospital Tomorrow*. There was a brief story beneath about the accident on the Sunshine State Parkway in which the girl was killed.

Baker lifted his eyes from the paper and whistled. "If this guy is the Stiletto," he said in a sober voice, "he's goin' to be a tough one to nail down. He doesn't believe in leaving any witnesses around. Either his own or someone else's!"

10

Baker stood in front of the automobile showroom on Park Avenue. Through the windows the sleek foreign cars shone with their highly polished newness. Lettered simply in small silver block letters on the glass entrance doors were the words: *Cesare Cardinali, Imported Automobiles.*

He opened the door to the showroom and walked in. There were several customers looking at cars and he stood around for a few minutes. One of the customers left and the salesman came toward him.

He was a tall silver-haired man and wore a morning coat and a small flower in his buttonhole. He looked more like a stockbroker than an automobile salesman. "Can I help you, sir?" His voice was inquiringly polite yet somehow aloof.

Baker smiled to himself as he thought of the difference in the approach to a customer here and at the Smiling Irishman where he had bought his car. He shook his head slightly. "I would like to see Mr. Cardinali." He asked, "Is he around?"

A disapproving look came over the salesman's face. "Mr. Cardinali never comes into the showroom," he said haughtily.

"No?" Baker smiled. "Then where can I find him?"

"I'm sure I don't know," the salesman answered. "But you might try the office."

"Where is that?" Baker asked gently. He had long since learned not to be annoyed by snobs. Too many of them proved empty shells once their props were removed.

"On the fifteenth floor. You can get the elevator in the lobby through that door." The salesman indicated an entrance on the side.

"Thank you," Baker said.

"Not at all," the salesman replied, walking politely toward another prospect who had just entered the showroom.

Baker walked into the lobby and waited for an elevator. This was one of the new buildings on Park Avenue. Everything was automatic, even the elevators had music piped into them. Cardinali was for real, he thought. He had it made. What could it be that tied a man like this to the Syndicate?

He remembered the incredulous expression on Strang's face when they had gone over the I.D. report.

"I don't get it," the captain had said. "This guy's got everything. Title. Money. War hero. Fame. Where does he fit in with the mob?"

That was the question that bothered them all. And

there were the soft points that bothered him. The soft edges around the hard facts that reached out toward something that could not be explained factually. For example there was the war record. Cardinali had co-operated with the Allies in the undercover job prior to the invasion of Italy and had received a medal for it. Still he had killed five of his contacts on that mission while all the others on the same mission, and there were more than twenty agents, found it necessary to eliminate only four people among them. Then there was the matter of Cardinali's uncle who had been murdered. Of course, Cardinali had been far away but soon after, though he had been broke at the end of the war, he began to make it big. There were the fast cars and the races, and in almost no time at all Cardinali had become a figure in international society. True, there were others like him. De Portago who was killed in that race. Cesare had been in that race too. He had been set down for unnecessarily reckless driving. There had been other races too where he had been set down. Twice the implication had been that he was responsible for the deaths of other contestants. But nowhere was there any clue that pointed to a connection with the underworld.

The elevator doors opened and Baker came out into a softly lit reception room around whose walls were prints of famous automobiles. The receptionist sat at a small desk in the far corner.

"Can I be of help, sir?" she asked.

Baker nodded. "I would like to see Mr. Cardinali."

"Do you have an appointment?" the girl asked.

Baker shook his head.

"May I have the nature of your business?" the girl asked.

"It's personal," Baker answered.

Disapprovingly the girl picked up the telephone. "I will see if Count Cardinali is in," she said haughtily. "Your name, please?"

"George Baker," he replied.

He stood there waiting while the girl whispered into the telephone. After a moment she looked up at him. "If you will be kind enough to take a seat, Miss Martin, Count Cardinali's secretary, will be out to speak with you in a few minutes."

He walked over to a comfortable couch and sat down. The table in front of him was covered with sports car magazines in every language and from every country. Idly he picked one up and began to glance through it. He looked up when a girl came through a door and stood in front of him.

"I'm Miss Martin," the girl said, smiling politely, "Count Cardinali's secretary. He doesn't see anyone except by appointment. Can I be of help to you?"

He got to his feet slowly, aware of the curious gaze of the receptionist. Silently he reached into his pocket and took out his identification. He gave it to Miss Martin.

She glanced down at it and then up at him, a puzzled expression crossing her face.

"I'm sorry to trouble the Count," he said reassuringly, "but there are some matters in which he may be able to assist us."

Miss Martin gave him back the small identification case and he put it in his pocket. "If you'll be kind enough to wait a moment more, I will see if an appointment can be arranged for you."

She disappeared through the door and he sat down again. A few minutes later she reappeared. "Follow me, please."

He followed her into a large working office. There were several girls and men working at desks there. The usual business office. Through that he entered another office. There was only one desk there. She led him past the desk into another office. This belonged to Cardinali.

Baker's eyes widened as he took in the furnishings. The antiques were authentic, the lamps of genuine statuary. Even the artificial fireplace was of fine Italian marble. On the mantelpiece over the fireplace were some awards and gold cups that were the only concession to commercialism in the entire office. Cardinali did not sit at a desk. There was no desk anywhere in the office.

He rose from a comfortable lounge chair next to a small telephone table with a note pad beside the telephone. He held out his hand to Baker. His grip was firm.

"How can I be of help to you, Mr. Baker?" he inquired, waving him to the seat opposite him.

Baker waited until the secretary left the office and then sat down. He studied the man opposite him for a few moments.

Cardinali took the scrutiny well. His expression remained even, a smile faintly on his lips. He seemed no more than politely curious over the reason for the visit. That fitted too, Baker found himself thinking.

Any man who had done what the Stiletto had needed nerves of ice. He smiled slowly.

"You are smiling?" Cesare asked.

Baker nodded. The thought had just jumped through his mind. Everyone had approached him since he had come here with a stock phrase: *Can I be of help to you?* Even Cardinali. And it had been his experience when there was so much overt helpfulness offered, there would be very little actually given.

"I was just thinking, Mr. Cardinali," he said, "how much more comfortable your office is than many I have been in. It seems almost too comfortable to be an inducement to work."

Cesare smiled. "Actually that is true," he admitted. "But in my line of work I do not find it necessary to disturb myself with the mechanics of business. So I keep my office as little like one as I possibly can. Mainly because I am a very selfish creature who is rather fond of his comforts."

Baker nodded. Everything this man said and did was exactly right. There would be no point in beating around the bush with him. Cardinali could keep this up all day. He leaned forward in his chair. "I trust you are well recovered from the effects of your recent accident?"

Cesare nodded. "I am quite well, thank you."

"It must have been a shattering experience," Baker prompted.

"It was more than that," Cesare said with a strange sort of earnestness as if he were seeking words in English to describe it. "It was tragic. I shall never stop blaming myself for allowing it to happen."

"You could have prevented it?" Baker asked quickly.

He thought he caught a glimpse of mockery deep in Cesare's eyes. "I think so," Cesare answered. "I should never have let her drive. The car was too much for her."

It was at that moment that Baker knew he had it, the answer to a great many questions. He had wanted Cesare to bait him into a direct probe and had succeeded, without revealing any of his own suspicions.

"I'm glad you're over it," Baker said quietly. "Now if we may get down to business?"

Cesare nodded. "By all means."

"As a result of the accident," Baker said, "it has come to our attention through the newspapers that during the past week you spent some time at the Maharajah in Las Vegas and the St. Tropez in Miami Beach."

"That's true," Cesare confirmed.

"And that also on Monday of last week you were in the Federal Courthouse in Foley Square here in New York?"

"Your people are very thorough," Cesare said. "That is also true."

"Do you have any idea why I'm referring to these places?" Baker asked.

Cesare smiled. "I would be a fool if I pretended ignorance, wouldn't I?" he asked. "I read the newspapers also."

"You are aware then of the murders of the witnesses in the trial of the criminal syndicate?"

Cesare nodded. "I am. But what I do not see is how I can be of help to you in connection with them."

Baker looked at him. "What were you doing in the courthouse that day?"

Cesare met his gaze. "You do not know?" He laughed shortly. "I went there to get my first citizenship papers."

"Immigration is on the ground floor," Baker said. "Yet you were observed on the third-floor corridor outside the courtroom."

Cesare laughed again. "That is simple enough too. You see the lavatory on the ground floor was occupied. I was told there was one on the third floor so I went up the staircase to it. When I saw the crowds I came downstairs again."

"You didn't notice anything unusual while you were on the third floor?" Baker asked.

"The whole thing was unusual to me," Cesare answered. "If you refer to anything particular, an incident, no. There was just the crowd and the men coming off the elevator and my trying to push my way through them to get back to the staircase."

"What reason did you have for going to these hotels particularly? Why not any of the others in Vegas or Miami?"

Cesare looked at him. "Hotels, Mr. Baker, are a matter of fashion. And in my business I have to be aware of such things." He took a cigarette from a box on the table next to him. "It would seem to me more relevant to ask the same question of the one responsible for allowing those witnesses to stay in those hotels."

"You never saw any of them?" Baker asked.

Cesare lit the cigarette and shook his head. "Not to my knowledge. Besides if I had seen them I would not have recognized them. I did not even know what they looked like." He hesitated a moment. "Perhaps in Vegas I saw one of them. I do not know. But as Miss

Lang and I were leaving the casino, a man was carried out, past us."

"That was one of the witnesses," Baker said.

"It was?" Cesare asked politely. "Too bad I did not know then. I would have perhaps looked more closely."

"Is there anything at all that comes to your mind that might be of help to us? Other people that you may have noticed?"

Cesare shook his head. "I'm sorry, Mr. Baker," he said regretfully, "there is nothing I can think of. You see, I was on a holiday with a very beautiful woman and I'm afraid I wasn't very interested in anything else."

Baker recognized the end of the road. The interview was over and nothing had been learned. And it wouldn't do any good to try to sweat it out of this man either. He wasn't the type. Baker got to his feet. As he did he saw a pair of crossed daggers mounted on the wall behind Cesare. "What are those?" he asked.

Cesare didn't turn around. "They are stilettos," he answered.

Baker walked over to the wall and looked at them. They were dull with patina. "Stilettos," he said. "The witnesses were killed with that sort of weapon."

"So I have read," Cesare said imperturbably.

"Have you had them long?" Baker asked.

"They are family heirlooms," Cesare answered. "I have quite a collection of them, here in New York in my apartment and at home in Italy. The stiletto was a favorite weapon of the Borgias who are listed among my ancestors."

"I see," Baker said. "I suppose you are an expert in their use."

Cesare got up smiling. "I suppose I am," he answered. "But there is not much room in our society to become really proficient at it. Weapons, like many other things, also are subject to the whims of fashion." He came over to Baker and took one of the stilettos down from the wall. He looked at it for a moment then handed it to Baker.

"Those little toys we market downstairs in the showroom kill more people in a month than all the stilettos made since they were first adapted from the Florentine."

Baker looked down at the delicate blade in his hand, then up at Cesare. A vague memory ran through his mind. "Are you the same Cardinali who was once fencing champion of Italy?"

Cesare nodded. "Another of the ancient sports I enjoy. Do you fence?"

"I did," Baker replied. "I was on the team at college." He put the stiletto down on the telephone table gently. "I must be going now," he said. "Thank you very much for your co-operation, Count Cardinali."

"I'm sorry I couldn't have been of more help," Cesare replied politely.

The stiletto was still on the small telephone table when Miss Martin came in to the office after Baker had left. She looked down at the stiletto then up at Cesare. "What did he want?" she asked with a familiarity born of long association.

Cesare picked up the stiletto and replaced it on the wall. He turned to her, smiling. "It seems I was very unwise in choosing the route for my holiday," he said.

Baker leaned back in his chair. "I didn't learn a damn thing," he admitted.

Strang smiled. "You didn't think you would, did you?"

Baker shook his head. "I guess I didn't. The only thing I did was convince myself. That guy is the Stiletto. I know it."

"Knowing it and proving it are two different things," Strang said.

Baker leaned over his desk and came up with several photographs of a wrecked car. He pushed them over to Strang. "Look at them. They were sent up from Florida."

Strang looked down at them. "Well?"

"See how the girl is wedged in behind the wheel? See how the motor was pushed back almost to the front seat through the dashboard? Well, if Cardinali was asleep like he said he was when the crash happened, where in hell were his feet? Not on the floor under the dash like you would think they were, or he never would have gotten out of that car. His legs would have been crushed when the front end came in on him."

"I've seen enough automobile accidents to know anything is possible," Strang said.

"Maybe," Baker admitted. "But I'm willing to bet my shirt right now that Cardinali had his feet on the seat under him until almost the moment the car hit and then he jumped."

"But what about the girl?" Strang asked. "She was driving."

Baker looked at him. "The only thing we're sure of is that she was behind the wheel."

"You still can't prove anything," Strang said.

"Right now I can't," Baker said. "But I have some ideas."

"Going to put a tail on him?" Strang asked.

Baker shook his head. "It would be wasted. In the circles in which that guy moves anyone we could put on him would stick out like a sore thumb. Besides it would make too much of a stink. You know how careful the chief is with important people."

"Then what are you going to do?" Strang asked.

Baker smiled. "The first thing is to leak to the newspapers that he was questioned. The next thing to do is to find someone that will stick close enough to him to maybe learn something and be of real help to us."

"Like who?" Strang asked.

"Like a dame," Baker said. "He's quite a ladies' man. Well, we're on to one that will fit right in. Society. Racing cars. The works."

"If he is the Stiletto, it might be dangerous for her," Strang said.

"She says she can handle him," Baker answered. "And I've had a look at her record and, believe me, if she can't, then nobody can."

11

The party was in full swing when Cesare entered the stateroom. He stood in the doorway, his eyes searching for the hostess. She saw him at almost the same time as he saw her and came hurrying forward, her hand outstretched.

"Cesare, my dear boy," she said, as he kissed her hand. "I'm so glad you could come."

"I would sooner die than miss Madame's sailing." He smiled.

She smiled, her somber eyes glowing under the rich gray hair. Her voice lowered and assumed a tone that was much like the voice Cesare had heard on the telephone just a few weeks ago. "This stateroom is next to his," she whispered. "There is a connecting door between the two bathrooms. He should be aboard in about ten minutes."

He didn't speak and she raised her voice as another guest approached. "And thank you for the lovely flowers."

"It is a pleasure, Madame," he answered.

He watched her turn to the other guest and move away. Once she had been a very beautiful woman, one of the most famous in international society. Her name still conjured up visions of glamorous ballrooms and princes. But now, she belonged to Don Emilio.

He moved toward the bathroom door slowly. He heard her laughter as he opened the door. How many more like her were there who walked the borderline of the two worlds? For that matter how many more were there like himself?

Emilio Matteo put his coat up against the wind that blew in from the chilly Hudson River as he got out of the taxicab in front of the pier. He looked up at the ship morosely as the detectives got out beside him. Without speaking, he gave one of them a bill for the driver.

"This way," the detective said and started for the pier.

"I know the way," Emilio said sourly. They walked onto the pier and over to the gangplank.

The little steward led them down a corridor on the first-class deck. Sounds of merriment came from behind the doors where bon voyage parties were almost at their height. The *Italia* was due to leave in less than an hour. The steward opened a door.

"This way, signore." He bowed.

Emilio entered the suite and the detectives fol-

STILETTO

lowed him. There was a small bar set up in the corner of the room.

The steward came in after them. "Is everything to the signore's satisfaction?" he asked Emilio.

Emilio gave him a bill. "Fine," he said.

The steward bowed again and left. The two detectives looked around. The oldest turned to Emilio. "This is pretty snazzy, Matteo," he said.

Emilio smiled at him. "Nothing but the best," he said, crossing to the bar. "You didn't think I would stay in one of those lousy cabins the government pays for, did you?"

The detective grinned. "I guess not."

Emilio opened a bottle and poured himself a drink. He threw it down his throat. "Ah," he said, "that's good whisky. It warms you up a little after that cold wind on the docks." He turned to the detectives. "Have a drink?"

The detectives looked at each other and smiled. "Don't mind if we do," the oldest said, walking over to the bar.

"Help yourself." Emilio pushed the bottle toward him. He took off his overcoat and threw it on a chair. "I guess I'm getting old all right, my kidneys ain't what they used to be. I'm going to the john."

He opened the bathroom door. The younger detective was at his side. Emilio stepped back. "Age before beauty," he said sarcastically. "Maybe you'd better have a look first."

The detective looked inside the bathroom. He turned back, a sheepish expression on his face. "Okay," he said.

"Thank you," Emilio said with formality. He stepped into the bathroom and began to close the door. "For some things a man must have a little privacy."

The door closed behind him and a burst of noise came into the stateroom from the cabin next door. "Sounds like a wild party," the younger detective said, pouring himself a drink.

"All it takes is money," the other said. He held his drink up in the air. "Shalanta."

"Shalanta," the other man replied. They swallowed their drinks. "This is good whisky," he added.

The other detective looked at him. "Like Matteo says," he said in a bitter voice, "nothing but the best."

The younger man stared at him. "Yeah," he said sarcastically. "Crime doesn't pay."

Emilio walked over to the sink and turned on the tap. He waited for a moment and listened. He could hear the faint murmur of the detectives' voices from his room. Quickly he crossed to the far end of the bathroom. There was a door there that connected with the next suite. It was locked.

He ran his fingernails against the door, making a scraping sound. "Cesare!" he whispered.

A scraping sound came back to him. Quickly he turned and opened the medicine cabinet. On the top shelf was a key. He put it in the door and turned it. The tumbler on his side clicked. A moment later he could hear the tumbler fall on the other side.

The door opened slightly and Cesare slipped into the room quickly and shut the door behind him.

Emilio smiled. "Don Cesare! My nephew!"

Cesare smiled also. "Don Emilio! My uncle!"

The two men embraced. "It has been a long time," Emilio said.

"A long time indeed," Cesare answered formally.

"You have done well, my nephew," Emilio whispered. "I am proud."

"I have kept the oath, Don Emilio," Cesare replied.

"You have, and the family will be pleased when I tell them of you. It is time now that you take a place in our councils."

Cesare shook his head. "I am content only to keep my agreement with you, Don Emilio. I seek nothing from the Brotherhood."

An expression of surprise came into Emilio's face. "You will have riches you never dreamed possible!"

"I do not need the riches," Cesare replied. "I have more than enough for my needs now."

Emilio shook his head. "The Dons will take this as an affront."

"It is not intended as such," Cesare said quickly. "You will explain this to them. I will repay my debt as I am called upon to do so, but no more."

"Already the other three men who were with me in the trial have petitioned the council for your death!" Emilio said. "They feel that you are a danger to them as long as you are free. And they have read in the papers that you have been questioned by the authorities."

"They are old women," Cesare said scornfully. "The police have learned nothing."

"But they are still worried."

"Explain to the council there is nothing to fear. There is nothing I want from any of them."

Emilio shook his head. "I will do as you ask, my nephew. But until you hear from me, be careful. They are dangerous men."

"I will be careful, Don Emilio." Cesare smiled. "For their own sakes I trust they too will be careful."

"I will get word to them," Emilio said.

Cesare nodded. "Good. And when will I hear from you?"

"Next month," Emilio answered. "I will bring word to you of the council's decision at the Gran Mexico sports car races. You will enter your Ferrari. Your mechanic will be detained in Italy and when you arrive in Mexico City the day before the race, you will receive a telegram that he is ill. You will hire one that I will send you. Then you will receive further instructions."

Cesare nodded again. "If there are any changes in my plans I will leave word for you at the restaurant of the Quarter Moon in Harlem as before."

Emilio smiled. "It is understood." He embraced Cesare again and then took his hand. "I will die for you," he said.

Cesare stared at him for a moment, then he replied, "I will die for you." Swiftly he turned and slipped out the door.

Emilio heard the tumbler click. He turned the key on his own side and put it back into the medicine cabinet. Then he turned off the tap and started back to his room, shaking his head. Cesare had signed his own death warrant by refusing further alliance with the Brotherhood. Now, he too must seek Cesare's death. Too bad he did not have the time to let the others know of his change of heart.

STILETTO

There is a restaurant in Manhattan on Lexington Avenue where the steaks are reputed to be the finest obtainable anywhere in the world and the spaghetti better even than in the old country. It is only natural in such a fine restaurant that the prices are so high that someone wandering in from the street could ill afford to have even bread and butter served to him. It is also only natural that the only customers who can afford such a restaurant either live on an expense account or have cash in such sufficient amounts that if necessary they could use the crisp new bills they love to carry in the large green salads served to them with spicy dressings.

Big Dutch stuffed a large piece of rare steak into his mouth and chewed on it. A tiny dribble of gravy slipped out of the corner. He swabbed at it with a piece of bread and pushed the bread into his mouth along with the meat. He chewed a moment more then looked over at his two companions. "I don't care what any of youse guys say," he mumbled, "I say we should hit him."

Allie Fargo stared at him. "But we ain't even sure he's the right guy. Emilio never came right out and told us."

Big Dutch swallowed his mouthful. His knife began to cut another piece of steak. "What difference does it make?" he demanded. "We ain't got time to check him out. The newspapers already said the F.B.I. has questioned the guy. Then what happens to us if he starts to sing?"

Dandy Nick looked down at his plate with distaste. This much food was wasted on him. He didn't eat very much anyway. "I don't like it," he said. "Emilio said we should sit tight and wait word from Italy. He's takin' it up with Lucky and Joe."

"Emilio says, Emilio says," Big Dutch burst out angrily, his mouth still filled with food. He swallowed quickly and went on. "I'm getting tired of what Emilio says. Them guineas sit over there on their fat asses while we stay here stickin' our necks out! They think just because they started the business they still own it!"

Almost unconsciously, Dandy Nick looked around the restaurant to see if they had been overheard. His voice dropped to a whisper. "Take it easy! That kind of talk will only wind up getting you measured."

Big Dutch stared at him balefully. "How do you guys know that they ain't settin' us up? Maybe they're figgerin' for this guy to take over? You know how them guineas stick together."

Dandy Nick was silent. He looked at Allie. Allie was eating stolidly, his eyes on his plate. After a moment, Allie looked up. He put his knife and fork down carefully. "It'll make an awful big stink," he said softly. "This ain't no dock walloper in one of your phony unions, Big Dutch. This is a pretty important geister."

"Yeah," Dandy Nick added. "And if he ain't the Stiletto, we'll still be in the same boat. And we'll have to explain to Emilio anyway."

Big Dutch kept on eating. It was time they made the move anyway. The Italians had had it long enough. The organization was here anyway; all the work, all the money was here. It was time they cut loose from the Mafia. What could they do from three thousand miles away if nobody wanted to work with them?

114

"I say we don't wait. We hit him." He didn't look up. He kept on eating. In a way it was too bad that he was in jail when they turned Roger Touhy loose. Big Dutch had already arranged a meet. The boys would have gone with Roger against the Mafia.

Dandy Nick's appetite was completely gone now. He pushed his plate away from him. He knew what Big Dutch was thinking. He glanced over at Allie. From the way Allie was eating he could tell that he knew too. This was more than just hitting one guy. This could be the beginning of a revolution. And he felt too old to go through another war just now. "What would we tell Emilio?" he asked, hoping to stall the decision.

Big Dutch's eyes flashed up at him for a moment, then down at the food again. "We'll think of something," he said.

Allie came right out with it. "I don't know," he said. "Look what they did to Touhy. Twenty-five years they waited for him."

Big Dutch's voice was scornful. "Touhy went soft in the clink. He should've gone right to work. Things would've been different then. They were afraid of him. Remember how he had Capone buffaloed?"

"But they got him, didn't they?" Dandy Nick asked.

"Sure, but look how they did it," Big Dutch retorted. "With a couple of punk amateurs. The kids were so excited they even left the cop alive. All they can count on now is the punks who go for the reputation. Even this Stiletto guy. He don't belong. We got a business to protect. There ain't a top man in the country who won't go with us."

He put down his knife and fork and picked up the

steak bone in his fingers. He waved it at them. It was time they got off the fence. "I say we hit," he said emphatically.

Allie looked at Dandy Nick, then back to Big Dutch. There was no room nor time left for stalling. "Okay, we hit," he said.

They turned to Dandy Nick. His mind was already made up. The percentage was with the house, it was heads you lose, tails they win and all anybody could do was hope to stay on his feet until it was over. "Hit," he said.

Big Dutch smiled. It was only the first step but he had made it and they had gone with him. The Stiletto was only a symbol, it was the Mafia that was important. It was time they returned the country to the Americans to whom it belonged. Already his mind was busy redividing the take. The sums made his head spin. He got to his feet and looked down at them.

"I don't know about you guys," he said, "but this is the first night the old lady let me out of the house since I got back from the can and I'm going to Jenny's and get laid."

They didn't answer and he turned and started out of the restaurant. When he was gone they looked at each other. "Coffee," Dandy Nick told the waiter.

He turned back to Allie when the waiter had gone. Now was the time for them to take out an insurance policy. They had to get a message through to Emilio.

12

The weekly session of the Fencing Club was in full swing on the third floor of the New York Athletic Club on Central Park South. Through the small gymnasium that they used echoed the clash of foil upon foil as the white-shirted men danced back and forth, their grotesque black masks hiding their faces.

Cesare's foil flashed down in the white light and arced in past his opponent's guard, coming to a stop on the little red heart emblazoned on the white shirt.

"Touché!" his opponent said, stepping back and lifting his foil.

Cesare flipped up his mask. He smiled. "You did very well, Hank. You still must watch your wrist though. It is too loose."

The opponent lifted his mask. He was breathing heavily. He smiled back at Cesare. "Are you going to

117

enter the tournament next month, Cesare?" he asked.

Cesare shook his head. "I don't think so. I have entered the Gran Mexico races and probably will not be back in time. But, after all, it is for business, no?"

The man nodded. "Too bad though. We won't have much of a chance without you. Thanks for the lesson anyway."

Cesare nodded. "You are quite welcome." He turned to the small group of onlookers and grinned. "Who is to be my next, how do you call it, pigeon?" he teased.

They laughed a little self-consciously and looked at each other. "I guess you'll have to wait until Fortini gets here. You're out of our class," one of them said, referring to the fencing coach.

"All right, then," Cesare said. He began to take off his mask.

A voice came from the doorway. "How about giving me a chance?"

Cesare turned. Baker was standing there, in uniform, smiling. "Ah, Mr. Baker," Cesare said, no surprise in his voice, "of course."

Baker walked toward him, picking up a foil from the rack. He flicked it through the air, loosening his wrist. He transferred the foil to his left hand and held out his right hand. Cesare took it. Baker's grip was firm. "Count Cardinali," he said, "when I learned you were a member here, I could not resist the temptation—the chance to cross swords with one of the truly great fencers of our time."

Cesare smiled slowly. "I am honored. You are very kind. Would you like a few minutes to warm up?"

Baker nodded. "Thank you, no. I am about as good

as I ever will be. I only hope to give you a few interesting moments."

"I'm sure you will." Cesare smiled again. They moved out into the open space and took up positions. "I did not know you were a member here."

Baker smiled back at him. "I'm afraid I don't have very much time to spend. My work usually keeps me pretty occupied." He flipped down his mask. "Ready?"

Cesare nodded. He closed his mask. The foils crossed in mid-air. *"En garde!"* Baker called.

Baker lunged forward and Cesare deflected the thrust and stepped back. He knew at once that Baker was no ordinary amateur. He smiled beneath his mask. He waited for Baker to lead again. There might be some fun in this encounter after all.

People began to drift across the gymnasium. There was a curious kind of tension that was immediately felt in the room. Baker pressed forward with a furious kind of concentration. Cesare's foil flashed as he parried attack after attack. Slowly, step by step, he began to fall back. The onlookers began to sense an upset. A low murmur began to fill the room.

Baker still kept pressing forward. He was beginning to feel confident. Cardinali didn't seem to be anywhere near as good as his reputation. He slashed in and Cesare locked foils with him. Baker tried to free his foil but Cesare held him easily. Baker pushed with all his strength at the man in front of him. Cesare didn't move. It seemed to Baker as if he were pushing against a steel coil. Suddenly he realized that Cardinali had only been toying with him.

At the same moment Cesare pushed him away. Baker

119

fell back a few steps and recovered in time to block a simple thrust. He lunged forward in a feint, then turned his foil quickly. Cesare was waiting for him.

Cesare laughed. "Very good," his voice came patronizingly from beneath the mask. "Maestro Antonelli?"

"Yes," Baker answered, watching Cardinali carefully. "Rome, 1951."

"My compliments," Cesare said, beginning his attack. "Signor Antonelli is very careful about his pupils. He accepts only the best."

Baker was busy defending himself now. There was no time left for him to launch an attack. "Apparently I didn't spend enough time with him," he managed to say wryly.

Cesare laughed again. "The sword is a very demanding master. And in our time, as I said before, there are other weapons much more in fashion."

Cesare's foil seemed to suddenly have a life of its own. Baker could feel himself running out of breath. His own foil seemed to weigh a ton in his hand. Cesare seemed to sense his weariness and slowed down his attack.

Baker could feel the perspiration running down his face inside his mask. Each breath began to come more labored to his throat. Every motion was an effort now and still Cesare was moving gracefully, breathing easily. There were a dozen times he felt Cesare could have scored and each time Cesare purposely turned his foil away. A little more of this and he would fall exhausted to the floor.

His rising anger brought a wave of strength back to his arms. He summoned all his reserves for a last attack. He deflected Cesare's foil and thrust forward.

"*Touché,*" the sound came from the spectators.

Baker stopped suddenly and looked down. Cesare's foil was resting on his heart. It had come so quickly that he hadn't even seen it.

He lowered his foil and opened his mask. "You're much too good for me, Count Cardinali," he said, breathing heavily.

Cesare saluted him with his foil. "I am lucky that you do not have more time for practice," he said smiling.

Baker forced a smile to his lips. "Now, *you* are being kind."

"Perhaps you will join me in a drink, Mr. Baker?" Cesare asked.

"Thanks," Baker said quickly. "I could use one right now. I've had it."

They sat in front of an open fire in the lounge. Cesare's long legs were stretched out in front of him. He looked at Baker sitting opposite him and lifted his drink. "You did not come here merely to fence, Mr. Baker."

Baker looked at him. In some ways Cardinali wasn't very European at all. In this, for example, he came right out and spoke his mind. "That's true, Count Cardinali," he said. "Actually I've come to warn you and offer our help."

Cesare lifted an eyebrow. "That's very kind of you, but for what reason do I need warning?"

"We've had word downtown that your life is being threatened," Baker said.

121

Cesare laughed. "How very melodramatic!"

"It's not funny," Baker said. "Certain men want you killed."

"Me? What men?"

Baker looked at him. "Big Dutch, Allie Fargo, Dandy Nick."

Cesare's face was impassive. "Who are they?"

"The defendants in the trial where the witnesses were killed. You see, they think you're the Stiletto."

Cesare's laugh was genuine and clear. "In that case why should they want to kill me? If I am the one who saved their miserable lives?"

Baker leaned forward. "That's just it. They are afraid of you. They think you might turn against them."

"They are stupid," Cesare said, taking a sip of his drink.

"But they are dangerous," Baker said earnestly. "There is no protection against a bullet in the back."

Cesare got to his feet. "I can look after myself," he said shortly. "I have survived worse dangers in the war than those men. You must know that by now. I hear your office is very thorough."

Baker nodded. "Yes, but we would still like to be of help."

Cesare's voice grew cold. "Your office has been of all the help to me I want. Perhaps if you were not so eager to obtain publicity in the newspapers, these men would not even know of me."

Baker stood up. "We're sorry about that, Count Cardinali. I don't know how the newspapers got wind of our conversation, but if you should have any trouble don't hesitate to call on us." He held out his hand.

Cesare took it. "Thank you, Mr. Baker. But I don't think it will be necessary."

Cesare opened the door and entered the small foyer of his apartment. He began to take off his topcoat. "Tonio!" he called.

He stood there for a moment, then dropped his coat into a chair. He crossed to the kitchen door and opened it. "Tonio," he called again. There was no answer.

Shaking his head, he crossed back into the living room and walked toward his bedroom. He would have to do something about that boy, whether or not he was Gio's nephew. A servant should go only so far. Too often Tonio was not around when he arrived home. America had spoiled him.

He opened the door and walked into the bedroom. He turned on the light and started for the bathroom. The sound of running water came from it. He stopped. "Tonio!" he called again.

There was no answer. He started for the bathroom quickly, then stopped. Baker's warning flashed through his mind. He moved his hand and the stiletto appeared in it. Silently he stepped to the door and flung it open.

A girl was just stepping from the shower, a towel held in her hand. She stared up at him, a startled expression on her face. "Cesare!"

"Ileana!" His voice was an echo of her surprise. "What are you doing here? I thought you were in California!"

Ileana raised the towel to her bosom. "I am taking a shower," she said. Her eyes fell to the stiletto in his

123

hand. "What are you doing with that knife? Who did you think would be in your bathroom?"

Cesare let go of the stiletto and it disappeared into his sleeve. Ileana ran to him, threw a moist arm around him and kissed him, holding the towel with her other hand. "Oh, Cesare, I need your help!"

Cesare looked down at her skeptically. It wasn't Ileana who usually needed help. "What happened to your rich Texan?" he asked.

Ileana looked up at him. "You are angry with me," she said. "I can tell. Because I did not wait for you in Monte Carlo."

Cesare began to smile. "Ileana, you didn't answer my question," he said softly.

She turned away from him and went over to the dressing table and sat down before it. She looked up at his reflection in the mirror. "Be kind to me, Cesare," she said in a small voice. "I have gone through a terrible experience." She took a small towel from the rack and held it back toward him. "Please dry my back, I can never reach it."

He took the towel from her. "The Texan, Ileana. What about him?"

Her eyes were wide. "I don't want to talk about it. It was too horrible. Do you think I've lost weight, Cesare?"

He was smiling now. He began to pat her back with the towel. "You look all right. What happened?"

Ileana closed her eyes for a moment. "I am relieved," she said. "I was sure I had lost weight." She opened her eyes and turned toward him. "The Texan, he was married."

"You knew that." Cesare smiled.

"Of course," Ileana retorted. "I am not a child. But his wife was a horrible woman. Not very understanding. Really very provincial. She even reported me to the Department of Immigration. Do you know, Cesare, they are very stupid men?"

Cesare shook his head silently, still smiling.

"They could not understand," she continued quickly, "how I could live in this country eight years without money and without working. They said if I did not have a job or a source of income they would deport me on the grounds of moral turpitude."

Cesare put down the towel. "And what did you tell them?"

"What else could I tell them?" She shrugged. "I told them I was working for you. They did not believe it when I told them that I did not need a job in order to live. Cesare, would you give me a job?"

Cesare looked down at her. "I don't know." He smiled. "What can you do? You can't take dictation, you can't type. What will I use you for?"

She rose from the chair and turned toward him. She still held the towel precariously in front of her. Her eyes looked into his. "You are in the automobile business, no?"

Cesare nodded.

She moved very close to him. "There must be something I can do. I once owned a Rolls Royce."

He began to laugh. He held out his arms to her and she came into them and he kissed her. "All right, we'll see what we can do."

"You will, Cesare?" Her voice was excited. "You're wonderful!" She put her hands up to stroke his cheek. "I won't be any trouble to you, Cesare. I promise. I

125

only have to work long enough to get a social security number, I think they call it. That's all they need to convince them that I'm legitimate."

His arms tightened around her. "You're legitimate all right." He laughed. "You can always tell them I knew your parents."

She glanced up at him quickly to see if there were any hidden meanings in his words but his eyes were laughing. Something caught in her throat and for the first time in a long while, even as he kissed her, she thought of her parents.

She remembered the expression on her father's face the night he opened the door of her bedroom and saw them all in bed together. Her mother. Herself. And the rich American.

13

Her mother was English and only seventeen when she had married the dashing young Rumanian, Baron de Bronczki. The tabloids at the time had called it a storybook romance. Less than a year later Ileana had been born, there had been a revolution and the storybook was ended. Life has a way of dealing with romance.

Actually she never had much of a chance to know her parents while she was a child. She had a vague idea that her mother had been a very beautiful girl and her father a very handsome man, but she had spent most of her life in schools away from them.

First there had been that school in England. She had gone there when she was almost five years old when the war had begun. Her father had gone into the

British Army and her mother was wrapped up in the wartime social frenzy and had no time for her.

Then when the war was over they had moved to Paris and she had been sent to a school in Switzerland. The excuse then was that her father, almost a cripple now from his wounds, would be too occupied with his struggle to regain his lands and former wealth to let them settle permanently in any one place. It never occurred to her to question her mother on her feelings about it. Her mother was always too busy with her friends and social activities. Besides there was something about her mother that made Ileana feel too awkward and out of place to dare speak with her.

Ileana was almost fourteen then and the school in Switzerland was different from the one in England. In England the emphasis had been on the academic, in Switzerland the emphasis was on the social. The school was filled with rich young ladies who had been sent from England and America to have superimposed on their youthful freshness a finishing polish that was available nowhere else in the world. Ileana learned to ski and swim and ride. She also learned how to dress and dance and make small talk.

When Ileana was sixteen, she had already begun to fulfill the promise of her beauty. Her complexion and eyes were English, her figure and grace came from her father. And right across the lake from her school was a similar school for young men. Close contact was kept between the two schools for they needed each other to complement their work.

There had been an outing that summer when she turned sixteen. Her partner had been a tall dark young man who was heir to some throne in the

STILETTO

Middle East. He had a long name that no one could remember so they called him Ab, short for Abdul. He was a year older than she, and darkly aquiline, blue-eyed and handsome. Their canoe had taken them to a small island away from the others and now they lay, stretched out in their swimming suits on the sand, soaking up the bright midday sun.

He rolled over on his side and looked at her for a moment. She looked into his eyes and smiled. His face was serious, then he leaned over and kissed her.

She closed her eyes and put an arm up around his shoulder and held him closely to her. She felt good. The sand and the sun and the warmth of his mouth. She felt him open the straps of her thin bathing suit, then his fingers on her naked breast. A pleasurable excitement began to grow inside her. A bubble of happy laughter rose into her throat.

He raised his head and looked at her, still serious. The young strong breasts and awakened nipples. Slowly he traced them with his fingers and kissed them.

She smiled at him. "I like that," she said softly.

His eyes were unwinking as he looked at her. "You're still a virgin?"

She couldn't tell whether he was making a statement or asking her. She nodded silently.

"Why?" he asked her. "Has it something to do with your religion?"

"No," she answered. "I don't know why."

"They call you 'the cold one' in my school," he said. "None of the others in your class are virgins."

"That's silly," she said. She could feel her heart beginning to pound inside her.

He stared at her for another moment. "I think, then, it's about time, don't you?"

She nodded silently.

He got to his feet. "I will be right back," he said and walked down to the canoe.

She watched him go down the beach to the water's edge and reach into the canoe. She put her hands up under her bathing suit and pushed it down her legs and kicked it off. The sun felt good on her body. She turned her head to see what he was doing.

He had taken something from the pocket of his trousers and was walking up the beach toward her. He stopped when he saw her. He held something in his hand.

"What's that?" she asked.

He opened his hand so that she could see what he held in it. "So you won't become pregnant," he answered.

"Oh," she said, without surprise. Everything had been very carefully explained to them in school. It was part of the curriculum, one of the important finishing touches so their young ladies would be completely equipped to venture forth in the world. She turned her face away as he slipped out of his trunks.

He knelt in the sand beside her and she turned back to him. She stared at him for a moment. Her voice filled with wonder. "You're beautiful," she said reaching for him. "Beautiful and strong. I never knew a man could be so beautiful."

"Men are naturally more beautiful than women," he said matter-of-factly. He bent to kiss her. "But you're very beautiful too."

She pulled him closer to her, a sudden demanding

fever leaping in her veins. Unexplainably she began to tremble.

He raised his head, thinking she might be frightened. "I'll try not to hurt you," he said.

"You won't hurt me," she said hoarsely, aware now and knowing of the capacity for delight within her. "I'm strong too!"

And she was. Much stronger than she thought. It took a doctor in Lausanne to complete her defloration on the surgical table.

She was eighteen when she appeared at the door of the de Bronczki apartment in Paris. Her education had been as complete as any girl in the school and in many ways she had surpassed most of the students because she was more beautiful and her capacities were greater. She pressed the bell and waited for the door to open.

Her mother opened the door and looked at her without recognition. "Yes?" she asked, in the tone of voice she kept for servants and inferiors.

Ileana half smiled to herself. She didn't expect much more from her mother. "Hello, Mother," she said in Rumanian.

A look of surprise came over her mother's face. "It's you," she said in a shocked voice.

"That's right, Mother," Ileana said. "May I come in?"

Flustered, her mother stepped back from the door. "We didn't expect you until next week."

Ileana picked up her suitcase and walked into the apartment. "I sent you a telegram last week." She asked, "Didn't you get it?"

Her mother closed the door. "The telegram. Oh,

yes," she said vaguely. "Your father did mention something about it before he left on a business trip."

For the first time Ileana felt a sense of disappointment. "Daddy's away?"

"He'll be back in a few days," her mother said quickly. "Something came up with his estate claims." For the first time she really looked at Ileana. "Why, you're taller than I am," she said in surprise.

"I'm all grown up, Mother," she said. "I'm not a little child any more."

Her mother's voice grew petulant. "For God's sake, Ileana, speak French instead of that horrible language. You know I never could understand it."

"Of course, Mother," Ileana replied in French.

"That's better," her mother said. "Now let me take a look at you."

Ileana stood very still while her mother walked around her slowly. She felt like a horse on the auction block.

"Aren't you dressed rather too old for your years, dear?" her mother asked.

"I'm eighteen, Mother. What did you expect me to wear? A middy blouse and skirt?"

"Don't be fresh, Ileana. I'm trying hard enough to get used to the idea of having a grown-up daughter. Why I don't look that much older than you that we can't be mistaken for sisters."

Ileana looked at her mother. In some ways, she was right. Somehow she had managed to keep an air of youthfulness about her. She didn't look her thirty-six years. "Yes, Mother," she said quietly.

"And stop calling me 'Mother,' " the older woman snapped. "It's old-fashioned anyway. If you must call me something call me by name. Or better still 'Dearest,' as your father does. Everyone calls me that now."

"Yes, Moth—Dearest," Ileana said.

Her mother smiled. "Now that wasn't so bad, was it? Come, let me show you your room."

Ileana followed her mother down the long corridor to a small room on the far side of the kitchen. No one had to tell her it was a servant's room. The furnishings did that very clearly.

"It will be quite nice when we fix it up," Dearest said. She looked up at Ileana. Ileana's face was impassive. "What's the matter?" she asked sharply. "You don't like it?"

"It's small," Ileana said. Her closet at school seemed larger than this.

"Well, you'll have to make do with it," Dearest snapped. "Your father isn't one of the wealthiest men in the world, you know. And its difficult enough to manage on the money we have as it is."

She started to leave the room and at that moment the doorbell rang. She stopped, then turned back to Ileana, a startled expression on her face. "Oh, I almost forgot. I have a cocktail date with an American friend of ours. Be a dear, will you, and get the door for me. Tell him I'll be ready in a moment."

She hurried back through the corridor, Ileana following her. At the door to her room, Dearest stopped and looked at Ileana. "And do me another favor, darling. Don't introduce yourself as my daughter this time. Tell him you're my sister and down for a visit. I don't feel quite up to involved explanations just now."

Dearest shut her door quickly before Ileana could

answer. Ileana walked down the hall and through the living room slowly. She didn't need anyone to draw a diagram for her. The school in Switzerland was very thorough.

When her father came home the following week, Ileana was shocked at the change in his appearance. The once tall figure was bent and stiff with the pain from his almost immobilized legs. He moved slowly with his canes and dropped into his wheelchair as soon as he was inside the door. He looked at her and smiled as she knelt beside him. He reached out his hand and drew her toward him.

"Ileana," he said. "I'm glad you're home at last."

In spite of his infirmity, the Baron had to spend a great deal of time away from home. There was the matter of his estate to be settled, a negotiation was pending with the present regime that would allow some sort of compensation for their losses to the former holders of property. Return was impossible for now the country was firmly in the Soviet bloc.

During the times her father was away, Ileana busied herself with friends. She kept out of the apartment as much as possible and very often used the back door when she heard voices in the living room.

It was more than a year later that she received a letter from a school friend inviting her to spend the summer with them in Monte Carlo. The Baron was away again and she hurried to her mother's room with the letter. Excitedly, she gave the letter to her mother.

She spoke while her mother was reading the letter. "It will be so wonderful, just to get away from Paris in the blistering heat. The beach and the water. I just can't wait!"

STILETTO

Dearest folded the letter and put it down on the table. "You can't go," she said. "We can't afford it."

"I can't?" Ileana's voice was incredulous. "But I won't need any money. I'll be their guest."

Dearest looked up at her. "You'll need clothes," she said. "You can't go looking like a ragpicker."

"I have clothes," Ileana flared up. "Everything I had from school still looks well on me."

"But the styles have changed and they're dated," Dearest said. "And everyone will know you couldn't afford a proper wardrobe. Drop her a note and explain that unfortunately you've made other arrangements. You can use my stationery if you like."

"Save your crested stationery!" Ileana said, close to tears. "I have my own." She stamped out of the room.

While she was still in the corridor, the front door-bell rang. Dearest's voice floated after her. "Get the front door for me, darling. I'll be out in a minute."

Clenching her teeth, Ileana went to the front door. It was another one of Dearest's American friends. He was already slightly drunk. Ileana introduced herself as Dearest's sister.

He came into the apartment and sat down on the couch. He looked up at her. "The Baroness never told me she had such a beautiful sister."

Ileana laughed at his typically American attempt at gallantry. "My sister never told me she had such an attractive friend."

He laughed, pleased with himself. "It's too bad I have to go back home tonight. Otherwise we might have become better acquainted."

Dearest's voice came from the doorway. "You have to return, John? Oh, I'm so sorry."

She came into the room and John struggled to his feet. "I was called back," he said sadly. "An emergency in the factory."

"That is too bad," Dearest said, taking his hand.

"It is too bad," he said earnestly, looking into her eyes. "Three times we had cocktails and dinner together and each time I said to myself it would be the next time. And now I have to go back and there will never be a next time."

"You will come back to Paris," Dearest said.

"Yes," he answered. "But who knows when?" He sat down on the couch again. He looked up at Dearest. "I stopped in the bar downstairs and had three whiskies before I came up."

Dearest laughed, her false tinkling laughter that Ileana knew so well. "What on earth for?" she asked.

His face became very serious. "I have something very important to ask you."

Dearest looked at Ileana. "Will you get some ice from the fridge, darling? John likes lots of ice with his whisky."

Ileana turned and left the room. She pulled the ice cubes from the tray and put them into a small serving bowl. When she came back into the room, John and her mother were both silent. She began to place the bowl on the small coffee table in front of the couch when she saw the pile of bills stacked on it. It was American money.

She glanced at John quickly. He didn't speak. He still held his wallet in his hand. She looked at her mother questioningly.

John saw the look. He spoke to Dearest. "I'll make it twenty-five hundred dollars if she joins in the party."

STILETTO

Suddenly she knew what he meant. She fled from the room, her face flaming, and closed the door of her room behind her.

A few moments later Dearest came into the room. Her face was cold and she looked down at her daughter. "Why did you run from the room like that?" she asked angrily. "It was absolutely infantile."

Ileana stared up at her mother. "But you know what he was asking, Mother. It was disgusting. He wanted us to go to bed with him."

"You don't have to explain it to me," Dearest snapped.

"You're not going to bed with him?" Ileana's voice was incredulous. "With that drunk?"

"I am," Dearest said calmly. "And so are you!"

Ileana sprang to her feet. "I will not! And you cannot make me!"

"Do you know how much money twenty-five hundred American dollars is? One and a half million francs on the black market. How do you think we have been living anyway? On the thirty-two pounds a month disability pension that your father gets from the army? How do you think we can afford the medicine and doctors for him? From the estates he will never see again? What kind of a life do you think it is for me to spend my days with a cripple who cannot walk and is no good for anything a man is supposed to be good for?" Dearest shook Ileana angrily. "With this money you can go to Nice to your friends, we can live for six months, your father can have that operation he has postponed so many times."

Ileana sank back into her chair. "I won't do it. I can't. The whole idea makes me sick to my stomach."

137

Dearest laughed scornfully. "What are you talking about? Don't make me laugh. You're no innocent little virgin. I know what went on at that precious school of yours. You'll do as I say or I leave right now and you can explain to your father why I won't live with him any more. See if he appreciates your actions then—or even if he believes you!" She turned and swept out of the room.

Ileana sat for a moment, then got up slowly and walked out into the corridor. She stumbled against a table in the dark hallway. Her mother's voice came from the living room.

"Is that you, Ileana?"

"Yes," she answered.

"Be a dear, will you, and fetch us some more ice?"

"Yes, Dearest," Ileana replied. Her mother's tinkling laughter followed her into the kitchen.

A faint sound made her bolt upright in the bed. She cast a quick glance at her mother. Dearest was sleeping, an arm thrown over her eyes to shield them from the light. The American lay next to her on his stomach, breathing stertorously.

There was the sound again. A faint squeak as if from the wheel of a rolling chair. A cold fear clutched at her heart. She reached out and touched her mother quickly.

Dearest sat up. She rubbed her eyes. "What, what?"

"Hurry, Mother," she whispered, "into the next room! Hurry!"

Dearest was wide awake now, her eyes frightened. She began to get out of bed then stopped. It was too late. The door was opening.

STILETTO

The Baron sat there in his wheelchair, looking at them. His face was white and impassive, his eyes were cold.

The American got out of bed, reaching for his trousers with trembling hands. "I—I can explain," he stammered.

The Baron's lips scarcely moved. "Get out!"

Frightened, the man ran from the room. A moment later they heard the front door slam behind him.

The Baron sat there in his chair, looking at them. They stared back at him, Dearest shrinking back against the bed, Ileana, leaning forward and holding a sheet to her bosom. At last, her father spoke.

His eyes tore at his wife. "It is not enough for you that I looked away from what you are, because I loved you once and somehow felt responsible for you. But do you hate me so much that you have to turn your own daughter into a whore?"

Ileana spoke. "Father, it was I who—"

Her father looked at her. His eyes were the saddest she had ever seen. "Put something on, Ileana," he said gently, "and go to your room."

Silently, she slipped into her robe and started through the doorway. He rolled back his chair slightly to let her pass and his hand brushed her arm. His hand was cold as ice.

She went out into the corridor and he rolled his chair into the room and closed the door behind him. She was almost at the door of her room when she heard the shots. She ran back and opened the door. She screamed. Her mother lay dead across the bed, her father in his chair, the gun still smoking on the floor near his outstretched fingers.

139

Her father left her no money but her mother left an estate of more than sixty thousand dollars. Ileana took the money and went to Monte Carlo and lost it all in a week. She felt better when the money was gone. Cleaner. Then she went to Nice and visited with her friend.

It was there she first met Cesare. He had placed second in the annual race. It was also there she found a new way to live. Like her mother, there was always some rich man who was willing to help her. And somehow when she realized how like her mother she had become nothing much mattered any more.

The only thing that mattered was today. And how much living she could squeeze out of it—or into it.

14

Cesare walked back into the living room. "Tonio!" he called.

Tonio appeared in the dining-room archway, a bag of groceries still in his arms. "Excellency!" he cried. "You are home early!" He lowered his voice to a conspiratorial whisper and looked meaningfully toward the bedroom. "The Baroness de Bronczki is—"

"I know," Cesare interrupted him. "I've already seen her. Where have you been?"

Ileana's voice came from the bedroom door. "I sent him out to get some things in for dinner. I thought it would be nice if we had dinner in tonight."

Cesare turned to look at her. She was wearing black-velvet toreador pants that clung to her body, a gold lamé blouse and gold shoes. "You did, eh?" he asked. "What made you think I want to eat in? How did you know that I didn't have plans to dine at El Morocco?"

She laughed, shaking her head. Her long black hair shone in the light as she came into the room. "Oh, no, Cesare. We couldn't do that. Not tonight."

"Why not?"

She looked up into his face. "I could not go to El Morocco in these clothes. And they are all I brought with me."

He stared at her. "All? Where are the rest of them?"

She put her arms up to his face and kissed his cheek. Then she crossed to the couch and sat down.

"Tonio, bring us some cocktails," Cesare said.

Tonio bowed, shaking his entire frame. "Yes, Excellency." He went back into the kitchen.

Cesare looked down at her. "What happened to the rest of your clothes?"

"They are in California," she said simply. "All I have with me are these—and the mink coat. The hotel manager was not very understanding either. He locked me out of my room when my credit was cut off by that woman. Fortunately I still had the return ticket to New York in my purse. So I came to the airport and here I am." She smiled up at him. "Wasn't I lucky?"

Before he could answer, Tonio was back in the room. "Cocktails, signore," he announced.

Tonio placed the silver coffee pot and the tiny cups on the small table in front of the couch and, bowing, went back into the dining room. Cesare heard him clearing away the dishes.

Ileana leaned forward and poured the coffee. He watched her. In some unfathomable manner, he felt good. He was relaxed. That was a good thing about her. There was no need for pretenses between them. They understood each other. That was one advantage of being European.

She held the coffee cup toward him. "Sugar?"

He shook his head and took it. He sipped at his coffee slowly. The slightly bitter espresso tasted good in his mouth.

"You are very quiet tonight, *mon cher*," she said in French.

"I am tired," he answered in the same language. "I have been very busy."

She came over and sat down next to him. She stroked his temples gently. "See," she said softly. "It is a good thing I decided that we should eat in, no?"

He nodded, soothed by the light touch of her fingers.

"We shall retire early," she continued. "I shall see that you rest well. I will take care not to disturb you. I will be very small in the bed."

He opened his eyes and looked at her. "Tomorrow, we shall make arrangements to get you a room in the hotel."

"That will not be necessary," she said quickly, still stroking his temples. "This apartment is comfortable. There is room enough."

He smiled. "Americans are different, Ileana. You know that. It will be better if we get you a room."

She kissed him lightly. "All right. Anything you say."

He sipped at his coffee. Tonio came back into the room. "Will there be anything else, Excellency?" he asked.

"No, thank you, Tonio. Good night," Cesare answered.

"Good night, Excellency." He turned to Ileana. "Good night, Baroness." He bowed.

"Good night, Tonio." She smiled and watched the little servant walk from the room. She turned back to Cesare and refilled his coffee cup. "I have just been thinking," she said. "We cannot eat in every night."

A smile began to come to his lips. He knew what was coming. His hand started for his pocket. "Of course," he said. "How much will you need?"

Her face grew thoughtful for a moment. "Since I will be working for you, it will be proper to get a small advance on my salary?"

He nodded, still smiling. "Absolutely proper. It is done all the time."

She smiled. "Good. I am relieved. Let me have one thousand, no, better make it two thousand dollars. You can deduct it from my salary."

"Two thousand dollars?" His voice was incredulous.

She nodded her head seriously. "I will try to make that cover everything. I will be very careful."

"What are you going to buy?" he exploded. "The House of Dior?"

"Don't make jokes, Cesare," she said. "Surely you don't expect me to go out in these clothes?"

He began to laugh. It was completely ridiculous. She really had no conception of money. "All right then. I'll give you a check," he said.

He crossed to the small desk and wrote a check, then brought it back to her. "This should do," he said, holding it out to her.

She took it from him and placed it on the coffee table. It was for twenty-five hundred dollars. She looked up at him. Suddenly she felt very sorry for him.

He was such a strange tortured man. She held out a hand to him and drew him down on the couch beside her.

"Thank you, Cesare," she said softly.

His eyes were somber. "It is nothing," he replied. "After all, we must stick together. We're the last remnants of a dying civilization."

"Don't talk like that," she said quickly. "You make everything sound so hopeless."

He looked at her and in his eyes she could see the emptiness of futility. The inexplicable sorrow welled up in her. She kissed him and her hand dropped to his thigh. Her fingers felt the quick response of his muscle to her touch. She tightened her grip.

"Come," she said gently, a peculiar maternalism stirring inside her. He was tortured as her father was tortured. "I'll help you to relax."

Of this one thing she was sure. She knew everything that could make a man forget. And make herself forget too.

Big Dutch, looking back through the rear window of the limousine parked near the corner, saw them come out of El Morocco. "Start your motor," he said to the driver.

The tall doorman signaled for a cab. Big Dutch saw Ileana say something to Cesare. Cesare smiled and shook his head at the doorman. They turned and began to walk up the block away from him.

He swore angrily. Four nights they had cased the job and every night they had taken a cab. "They're walkin'," he said. "Go up Fifty-Third. We'll try to pick them up on Lexington Avenue."

But when they turned north on Lexington and sped toward the corner, they shot right past them. Ileana and Cesare were on the far side of the street and just turning up Fifty-Third toward Park Avenue. Big Dutch caught a glimpse of them as they turned. "Damn it! We missed them!" He swore. "Get over to Fifty-Fifth and come down Park. We'll try to pick 'em up there."

The driver turned a white anxious face back toward him. "I don't like this, boss," he said nervously. "Maybe we better hit 'em another night." He turned forward just in time to miss colliding with a milk truck. The big limousine swerved up Fifty-Fifth Street.

"You keep your eyes on the road," Big Dutch snarled. "I said it's gonna be tonight."

He stared down the street impatiently as they waited for the traffic light on Park Avenue. It had to be tonight. His wife was blowing a fuse. He had been out every night casing this job and he didn't know if she would stand for another.

The light changed and the car began to move. "There they are," he said. They were just crossing the pavilion in front of the Seagram Building. They stopped to look at the lights playing on the fountain.

"Turn at Fifty-Second," Big Dutch said, reaching for the tommy gun on the seat beside him. "We'll hit him when he comes down the steps!"

The big car turned and stopped near the east corner. Big Dutch looked around. The street was deserted. He looked up at the pavilion. Cesare and Ileana were just strolling casually toward the near fountain.

He picked up the gun and lined them up in his sights. It would be a cinch. He smiled. If you wanted

146

a job well done, you had to do it yourself. There was no use in trusting the punk kids nowadays. They were always horsing around, never paying enough attention to business. Another moment and the couple would be just where he wanted them.

Cesare and Ileana reached the top of the steps next to the fountain. He had Cesare squarely in his sights. "Now!" he shouted and squeezed the trigger.

The driver stepped on the accelerator and the motor roared together with the gun. The submachine gun fired twice and jammed. He saw Cesare's face turn toward him in the lights from the building; at the same time, the car began to move.

Frantically he tried to clear the jammed gun. He stole a quick glance at the building in time to see Cesare pushing Ileana into the fountain and diving behind the small wall. He cursed, pulling the clear lever. It was no use.

By this time they were turning the corner at Lexington Avenue. Through the rear window, he saw Cesare pull the girl out of the fountain. Then they were hidden behind the buildings as the car raced down the street. Angrily he threw the useless tommy gun on the seat beside him.

The driver turned the car down another street. "Yuh get him, boss?" he asked over his shoulder.

"Nah!" Big Dutch growled.

The driver turned the car onto Third Avenue. "Where to, now, boss?" he asked almost cheerfully.

"Downtown to the union office," Big Dutch said. As he spoke there was a loud report and he grabbed for the gun in his pocket.

Almost immediately the big car began to bump and

lurch. The driver pulled over to the curb. "We got a flat," he announced.

Big Dutch stared at him for a moment. "So what else is new?" he snarled, getting out of the car. He flagged down a passing taxi.

"It was no use," he thought, getting into the cab. There were some nights that nothing went right.

15

"Are you all right?" Cesare asked, as he pulled her, dripping, from the fountain.

Her eyes were wide and frightened. "Cesare, those men were shooting at you?" she asked.

He glanced around quickly. People were starting to come out of the building. "Don't talk," he said, quickly moving her down to the curb and into a cab.

"The Towers, driver," he said. The taxi started and he turned to her. "Are you all right?" he asked again.

She was still dazed. "I'm all right," she answered automatically. She looked down at herself. "My new dress! It's ruined!"

He smiled grimly. "Don't complain. You were lucky."

She stared at him, a growing knowledge in her eyes. "Those men were shooting at you!" she said.

"I don't know," he answered sarcastically. "I didn't have time to ask them."

She began to shiver. He took off his coat and placed it around her shoulders. His eyes were cold and hard. "I don't want anyone to know about this. Understand? Anyone," he said harshly.

She nodded. "I understand," she said, trying to keep her teeth from chattering. Her hand sought his and a hint of sadness came into her voice. "Maybe you're in more trouble than I am, my friend," she said softly.

The taxi stopped in front of the hotel and they got out. The doorman looked curiously at Ileana as she walked into the building while Cesare paid the driver.

He held a twenty-dollar bill in his hand so that the driver could see it. "You never brought us here," he said.

The bill disappeared in the driver's hand. "I never even picked you up," he said cheerfully, driving off.

Cesare opened the door to her room. He stepped back to let her enter. "Get into something dry," he said.

She hesitated in the doorway. "Maybe I'd better go upstairs with you," she said. "I'm afraid to be alone tonight."

"No," he said quickly. Then he looked at her. It might be a good idea to spend the night with her. "Let me change my clothes too," he said. "Then I'll come back in a little while."

Big Dutch sat in his empty office in the Union Hall and stared at the bottle of whisky on his desk. He picked it up and poured himself another drink. From downstairs came the faint sounds of the morning check-off. He picked up the glass and swallowed the liquor. It burned its way down his throat.

Maybe the others were right after all. He was too big a man to go out on jobs like these. It was better to leave them to the punk kids even if they weren't as good as he was. They had less to lose.

Nostalgically he thought about his youth. They were the good old days. Everything was wide open then. You called a spade a spade, and if somebody crossed you, you went after them. You didn't have to wait for no lousy council to have a meet first and then decide what to do.

He remembered the time that Lep called him and Sam Vanicola down to the little speakeasy in Brooklyn. "I want you and Sam to take a little drive up to Monticello and burn Varsity Vic," he had said. "He's getting too big for himself."

"Okay, Lep," they answered and went over to the bar and got six bottles of whisky to keep them company on the long ride.

When they got outside, they had an argument over whose car to take. He didn't like Sam's Chevy and Sam didn't like his Jewett. So they compromised and heisted a big Pierce from in front of one of the mansions on Brooklyn Heights.

It was about a five-hour drive in those days and close to two o'clock in the morning when they pulled up in front of Varsity Vic's roadhouse. They had about three bottles of whisky left in the car.

They got out of the car and stretched. "Take a whiff

of this air," Sam had said. "It smells different than the city. Clean. Boy, this is the place to live."

He still remembered the crickets chirping as they went inside. The place was fairly crowded and the last floor show was on. They stopped in the doorway and looked at the girls dancing a variation of the Black Bottom on the darkened dance floor. "Hey! Look at that one!" he had chortled. "The third from the end. That's for me. Them boobs bounce around like rubber balls!"

"We ain't got the time for that," Sam had said, pulling him over to the bar. "We're workin'. Let's get another drink."

"Private stock," Sam ordered.

The bartender put the bottle of whisky in front of them. "What brings you guys up from the city?" he asked sourly.

"We were takin' a drive," Big Dutch answered cheerfully. "It was hot in town."

"It was plenty hot up here too," the bartender said.

"Gettin' plenty of action, I see," Sam said, leaning on the bar.

"Good and bad," the bartender said noncommittally.

"Is Vic around?" Sam asked casually.

"I ain't seen him tonight," the bartender replied, equally casual.

The number was over and the girls picked their way past the bar as they went back to the dressing rooms. He leaned over and jiggled the breast of the girl as she passed him.

She turned quickly and looked at him. "Fresh!" she said, smiling, and walked on.

152

"I can fix that for you," the bartender said meaningfully.

"I'll take you up on that sometime," he answered, looking after the girl.

He looked at Sam and nodded. Sam turned and started for the manager's office. The bartender bent over the button that flashed a signal into the room.

"I wouldn't touch that if I were you," he said, smiling genially.

Slowly the bartender straightened up. He came down the bar, polishing the top with his cloth. "It's none of my business anyway," he said. "I'm just the barkeep here."

"That's right," he agreed. "Just leave it like that." He walked off and joined Sam at the door to the office.

They went in. Varsity Vic was sitting behind his desk. He looked up. A smile crossed his face. "Come in, fellas," he said.

They closed the door behind them. "We got a message from the Boss," he said. "He wants a meet."

"Okay," Varsity Vic answered. He looked across the room at his bodyguard, who promptly got to his feet. "Just let me know. I'll come down whenever he wants."

"He wants right now," he said.

Varsity Vic stared up at him. "Make it tomorrow. I can't come right now."

They turned as if to start out. The bodyguard began to smile and put away his gun. Sam knocked him cold with one punch. They turned back to Varsity Vic.

"You know the Boss doesn't like to be kept waiting," he said.

STILETTO

Varsity Vic's face had been white as they walked out of the roadhouse with him between them. The bartender sourly watched them go and kept polishing the same spot over and over with his rag.

He had gotten into the back seat with Varsity Vic and Sam got into the front to drive. As soon as they had pulled away from the roadhouse, he picked up another bottle of whisky and pulled the cork with his teeth. He held the bottle toward Vic.

"Have a drink," he offered. "You look cold."

Varsity Vic shook his head.

"Go ahead," he urged. "This is good stuff. Not like that crud you sell back there."

Still Varsity Vic shook his head. When he finally spoke, his voice was thin and almost cracking. "I'll give you guys a grand if you'll let me out of this car."

Big Dutch had taken another swill from the bottle. He looked at him silently without answering.

"I'll make it two grand," Vic said quickly. "How much are you guys getting for this job anyway? A hundred? A hundred and fifty? Two grand's a lot of dough."

"You hear him, Sam?" he called.

"I hear him," came the reply.

"Got the dough on ya'?" he asked.

"Right here in my pocket," Vic answered, touching his jacket.

"Okay," he said. He looked around. They were out in the country now. There were no houses around. "Pull off the road, Sam," he called.

The car jounced to a stop on the soft ground. "Gimme the dough," he said.

Varsity Vic had taken his wallet out with trembling

hands. Quickly he counted out the money on the seat. "Two grand," he said. "You guys are lucky. That was all the dough I had on me." He held up the empty wallet.

"Yeah," he said, "we're lucky. Now get out."

Varsity Vic opened the door of the car and stepped out. He turned back to the car. "Thanks, fellas," he said. "I won't forget this."

"I'll bet you won't." Sam laughed, squeezing the trigger of his automatic.

The heavy 45-caliber slugs threw Varsity Vic about ten feet back into the bushes. They got out of the car and walked over to look at him. The body twitched and then lay still.

"Siphon some gas out of the tank and douse him with it," he said.

"What for?" Sam asked.

"Lep said, 'Burn him,' and when the Boss says something, he means what he says."

Then they sat on the running board of the Pierce and drank the remaining bottles of whisky while they watched the fire. When they went to start the car, they found that Sam had taken all the gas from the tank and they had to walk three miles before they could steal another car and get back to the city.

Big Dutch leaned forward on the desk and sighed. He poured another drink. The good old days. They were gone all right. Lep and Sam were gone too. Lep had gone to the chair and Sam had caught the knife in the pool.

He picked up his drink and looked at it. Everything looked like gold through a whisky glass. It was the guineas' fault. He never believed that Sam really would talk. Not good old Sam. Sam was his pal. But they killed him anyway. They were like leeches: once they got on your back, they never let go. But this time it would be different. This time he would show them.

He swallowed the drink and reached for the telephone. Might as well call the old lady and let her know he was on his way home. She would be mad enough anyway.

He was busy dialing and he didn't see Cesare opening the door.

It was just before dawn that she heard his key turn the lock. "Is that you, Cesare?" she asked.

His voice was flat and tense. "Yes."

Then he was at the side of her bed, stripping off his clothes in a violent kind of haste. He came into her bed, his body hard and trembling. He seized her breasts.

Pain and fear came up together inside her. "Don't be in such a hurry, Cesare," she managed to laugh. "One would almost think you're an American!"

16

Cesare was raising his glass of orange juice to his lips when Tonio came bustling in. "Mr. Baker to see you, Excellency," he announced.

Cesare nodded. "Show him in," he said. He drank his orange juice and got to his feet as Baker came into the dining room.

"Mr. Baker," he said. "I did not expect to see you so soon again. Do sit down and have some coffee."

Baker sat down and studied Cesare while Tonio filled a coffee cup and set it down before him. Cesare returned his gaze evenly. "I see you had a little trouble last night," Baker said.

"I did?" Cesare replied politely. "What makes you say that?"

"The morning papers," Baker said.

"I did not see them."

STILETTO

Baker looked at the folded newspaper next to Cesare's cup. "What's that?" he asked pointedly.

Cesare looked down at the table. He looked up again at Baker, a faint hint of a smile in his eyes. "*The Wall Street Journal.* It's the only paper I read. For business."

Baker could feel his face flush. He reached in his overcoat pocket and took out a copy of the *Daily News.* He spread it on the table in front of Cesare silently.

Cesare looked down at it. The half-page headline seemed to leap up at him:

STILETTO STRIKES AGAIN!
BIG DUTCH MURDERED!

Cesare looked up at Baker. He shrugged his shoulders. "I don't see what that has to do with me," he said. "I told you I didn't know the man."

"On page five there's another story," Baker said. "A little after midnight a man and a woman were shot at on Park Avenue in front of the Seagram Building. The woman fell into the fountain. They hurried away before they were recognized."

Cesare buttered some toast. "So?" he asked.

"This Baroness you came in with last night. The doorman said her dress was soaking wet."

"No one shot at me," Cesare said, adding some jam to the butter on his toast.

Baker sipped at his coffee. "That still doesn't explain how the lady got her dress wet."

Ileana appeared in the doorway behind him. "Why don't you ask the lady?" she said, coming into the room.

158

The men got to their feet. Cesare introduced them. "Mr. Baker is with the F.B.I.," he added.

Ileana's eyes widened. "Oh," she said. She turned to Cesare. "Are you in trouble?" she asked in a concerned voice.

Cesare smiled. "I don't think so. But Mr. Baker thinks some people are trying to kill me."

"How perfectly horrible!" she exclaimed. She turned back to Baker. "Is that why you want to know how my dress got wet?"

Baker nodded.

"It was very embarrassing," Ileana explained with just the right amount of dignity. "You see, we had been at El Morocco and I'm afraid I had a little too much champagne. That and the new shoes. I tripped and fell into a puddle. I had hoped no one saw me."

"Are you sure you didn't fall into the fountain at the Seagram building?" Baker asked.

Ileana looked at him. Her voice became very haughty at the implication that he might doubt her word. "Of that, I am most positive!"

"What did you do after that?" he asked.

"Count Cardinali took me to my room. It's in this hotel," she said.

"What time did he leave you?"

She looked at Cesare. He reached over and patted her hand reassuringly. "You don't have to answer that if you don't want to," he said.

She turned back to Baker. "Is it important?"

Baker nodded. "It's important," he said seriously.

She took a deep breath. "About an hour ago. When he left to breakfast here in his own suite," she said, looking into Baker's eyes.

Cesare got to his feet. His voice was still low but it had gone cold. "And now, Mr. Baker, don't you think you've asked enough questions for one morning?"

Baker rose. He looked down at Ileana. "I am sorry, Baroness, for any embarrassment I may have caused you but it is my job to ask these questions."

Ileana kept her gaze down on the tablecloth. She did not look up at him. "I understand, Mr. Baker."

He turned to Cesare. "I would still keep my eyes open if I were you, Mr. Cardinali. The rest of those men will be even more dangerous now."

"I will, Mr. Baker," Cesare said, still standing.

Tonio came bustling in. "Your new luggage will be ready in time, Excellency," he said to Cesare. "I will have it at the airport at four o'clock."

Cesare nodded. "Thank you, Tonio," he said in an annoyed voice.

Baker looked at him. "Going somewhere?"

"I have entered the Gran Mexico Road Race," Cesare answered. "It begins the day after tomorrow. My Ferrari is already there."

"I am going too." Ileana looked up. She was smiling. "It will be very exciting."

Baker looked from one to the other, then he smiled slowly. "Good luck," he said, starting for the door. "Drive safely."

Cesare waited until he heard the door close then turned and spoke angrily. "Why did you tell him you were going with me?"

Ileana smiled up at him brightly. "I was only trying to help, Cesare." Tonio appeared again in the doorway. "Just a half a grapefruit, please," she said to him.

160

Cesare waited until the servant had gone. "If I wanted you to go with me, I would have asked you!" he snapped.

Her eyes widened. "Oh! I did not understand. There is another woman. Forgive me, Cesare."

Tonio returned with the grapefruit. He placed it before her and left again.

"There is not another woman!" Cesare said angrily.

"In that case I will go with you then," Ileana said practically. She spooned up some grapefruit and looked up at him. "Besides I cannot afford to work for you. I spoke to your secretary just before I came up here this morning. She told me my salary was recorded at one hundred twenty-five dollars a week."

Cesare was seething now. "Just what did you expect to make? You cannot do anything."

"I haven't the faintest idea." She shrugged her shoulders prettily and looked down at her grapefruit. "But I need at least that much money every day." She put a spoonful of grapefruit in her mouth. "This is delicious."

He stared down at her, beginning to smile in spite of himself. That was what happened when you understood each other. She never said a word about lying to Baker for him. And she never would.

She looked up at him, smiling in the knowledge that she had made her point. "Besides," she added, "there are some very rich Texans I know who will be in Mexico City for the race."

17

The desk clerk at El Ciudad Hotel in Mexico City permitted himself a knowing smile. "The Baroness has a lovely suite right next to your own, Count Cardinali."

Cesare glanced at him as he finished signing the register. "That will be fine. Thank you."

"And we have been holding this telegram for you." The clerk took an envelope from beneath the counter and held it out to him.

Cesare took it and opened it as he walked back to Ileana. He scarcely looked at it. It was the expected message. "I have just received word," he said to her, "my mechanic is ill."

"I'm sorry," Ileana said. "Is it serious?"

"It means I will have to find a new mechanic," he answered. "I'd better go right over to the garage and see what I can do."

"All right," Ileana said. "Will you be long?"

"I don't know," he answered. "Better go upstairs and get settled. I may be a little while. I will join you for dinner."

The garage hummed with activity as Cesare came into it. Men were everywhere, going over the cars in last-minute preparation for the race. He walked through to the small office in the back.

The little old man came out of the office when he saw him. "Count Cardinali!" he exclaimed, a smile on his face. "It's good to see you again."

Cesare took his hand. "It's always good to see you, Señor Esteban."

"Your car is on the lower ramp, stall twelve," Esteban said. "I suppose you are anxious to have a look at it."

"I am, Señor Esteban, but I have a serious problem," Cesare answered. "My mechanic was taken ill and I must find a replacement."

A sober look replaced the smile on the old man's face. "That will be difficult, Count Cardinali. All the Ferrari men are spoken for."

"I know," Cesare said. "But we must do something. Otherwise I shall not be able to start in the race."

"We must not allow that to happen," Esteban said quickly. "Let me start looking for one at once. I will call you the moment I have news."

"*Mil gracias.*" Cesare smiled. "In the meantime I will be at the car. I will do as much as possible to get it ready."

He had been working on the white Ferrari about an

hour when he saw the girl approaching. She was coming directly toward him. He straightened up, admiring the trim figure she made in the white coveralls.

She stopped in front of the car. "Count Cardinali?" she asked. Her voice was low and pleasant.

He nodded, reaching for a cigarette in his jacket which was hung over the door of the Ferrari. "Yes?"

"Señor Esteban says you're looking for a mechanic." Her eyes were very blue.

"You know of one? Where can I meet him?" he said eagerly. He was already bored with the work. This was the part of racing that he did not like.

The girl smiled. "I am one."

His surprise showed in his voice. "But a girl? This race is no place for a woman. It is fourteen hundred miles!"

The smile disappeared from her eyes. She looked right at him. "I've driven that far when I've had to," she said quietly. "But we're not going that far."

Cesare stared at her. "No?"

She shook her head, the blond ringlets around her tanned face caught the light and sparkled. "It will not be necessary." She bent over the hood of the car and looked in at the engine. "Don Emilio has other plans," she whispered.

His eyes widened slightly. He had not expected a girl.

She straightened up, smiling again. She held out her hand man-fashion. "I'm Luke Nichols," she said.

They shook hands. Cesare studied her. "But do you really know Ferraris?"

Her smile broadened. "I should. I've raced them all over the world." She saw Esteban approaching over Cesare's shoulder. "Ask him."

Cesare turned. Esteban smiled. "I see you two have already met. That is good."

"But a girl in the Gran Mexico Race," Cesare said. "Who ever heard of such a thing?"

"You are very lucky, Count Cardinali," Esteban reassured him. "Señorita Nichols had many offers but she had already decided not to enter this race until she heard of your predicament. Last year she drove her own Ferrari."

Cesare turned back to her. "Your own car?" he questioned. "What happened to it?"

She shrugged her shoulders. "I didn't win. It was hocked to the hubcaps so it's gone now. I had hoped to pick up something down here, but no luck."

"All right," Cesare said. "You must be good if my friend, Señor Esteban, says so. Standard cut of the purse if we win. Five hundred if we don't."

"It's a deal, Mr. Cardinali." She smiled.

He reached for his jacket and put it on. "Tune her up and take her out for a road check. Have a full report for me at five o'clock. I'll be in the bar at El Ciudad."

"Okay," she said. She turned to Esteban. Her voice became very businesslike. "Would you make arrangements for me to use the number two pit, Señor Esteban? The one with the new electrical timer. The first thing I want to do is go over the wiring."

Esteban nodded and Cesare turned away and started up the ramp. When he reached the top of the ramp and looked back, she already had the car rolling toward the pit.

The light in the cocktail lounge of the El Ciudad came from hidden recesses in the wall that not only hid the lamps but also the light that came from them. Cesare was happy that he could see the drink on the table before him; there was no use looking at his watch to check the time, he was sure he couldn't see the dial.

The door opened and a shaft of sunlight split the gloom. Cesare looked toward it. Luke came in and stood there, her eyes adjusting to the dimness, trying to find him. He stood up and waved to her.

Smiling, she sat down opposite him in the booth. "They ought to give you miners' lamps when you come in." She laughed.

"It is dark," he admitted. The waiter came up. "Can we have a little more light before we go blind?" Cesare asked him.

"Of course, señor." The waiter reached across the table and pressed a hidden button on the wall. Immediately a soft light came into the booth.

"That's better," Cesare smiled. "What will you have to drink?"

"A daiquiri, please," she said.

The waiter went away. Cesare looked at her. "What do you think of the car?"

Something almost like sadness came into her eyes. "It's a wonderful car. Too bad. Under ordinary circumstances with a car like that, one could win this race."

The waiter placed her drink before her and left. Cesare lifted his glass. *"Salud!"*

167

"Luck!"

They sipped at their drinks and put them down. "There will be other races," Cesare said.

Her voice was expressionless. "I hope so." She looked around. There was no one near them. "I have connected a timing mechanism to the speedometer," she said in a low voice. "Exactly one hundred fifteen miles from our starting point, it will blow, wrecking your generator. We will then be two hundred ninety miles from the next check point so it will be about five hours before they find us. There is a small deserted house about a half mile from the road. We will go there and wait for Don Emilio." She picked up her drink again.

Cesare sipped at his own. "Is that all?" he asked.

"That's all," she answered.

Cesare studied her. She had changed into a light summer frock that left no doubt as to her femininity. It also served to make her look more like a young American coed than a woman involved with the illegal activities of the Mafia. He half smiled to himself. Don Emilio was full of surprises.

She began to feel uncomfortable under his scrutiny. He was different than the others she had met. Generally they were coarse men and overt in their manner. There was no question as to where they belonged. But she didn't quite fit him into the pattern.

"What are you staring at?" she finally asked. "Haven't you seen a girl before?" Almost as soon as the words were out of her mouth she felt the fool.

He smiled slowly. "I apologize for staring," he said. "I was just wondering why? A girl like you?"

"The money is good," she said coldly. "I told you I

168

wanted a Ferrari. This is the quickest way for me to get it." She took another sip of her cocktail. "But what about you? You don't need the money."

He laughed easily. "There aren't enough races like these. And life between them can become very dull if one does not keep occupied."

He signaled the waiter and they were silent until the man had placed fresh drinks before them. Then Cesare picked up his glass and looked into it. "It is too bad," he said regretfully. "This is one race I would like to win."

Luke sipped at her drink. "I know how you feel," she said, her face suddenly lighting up. "There's nothing quite like it. The speed, the danger, the excitement. You feel alive, everything inside you tingles, the whole world is churning inside your body."

"That's it! That's just it," Cesare said quickly. An almost boyish excitement crept into his voice. "I didn't think anyone else felt like that. It is like having everything you want in the world. All the money, all the power, all the women!"

Luke looked down at her glass. She felt almost shy. "I didn't know anyone else could feel like that."

He put his hands across the table on her own. She could feel the strength and power coming from them. She looked up into his face. It was intense and his eyes were glowing like a tiger's eyes in the night.

"It is as if I had never been with a woman before," he said softly.

A sudden fright came up in her. Not of him, but of herself. She knew too well what a man like him could do to her. She took her hands away quickly. "Let's keep it business, shall we?" she said as coldly as she could.

"We both know we cannot win."

His voice was still soft. "Why, Luke? We are here. Why must we keep it business?"

His eyes were deep magnets and she could feel herself beginning to swirl in their depths. The familiar fever began to rise in her loins, the familiar weakness seep down into her limbs. Why did it always have to be like this? Just when she had everything worked out. She felt the bitter resentment toward herself creep into her voice. "Because with you I'm a loser. I've met guys like you before. It's always the same. First thing you know you can touch the stars. Then, like that—" She snapped her fingers.

"Must it always be like that?"

She met his look steadily. "Always."

"And you are content to go through life without living because you are afraid of losing?" he asked, almost gently.

She was angry because he had unerringly put his finger right on it. "What do you want from me anyway?" she snapped. "Are you one of those men who have to gobble up everything in sight? Possess every woman? You're here with a woman who can probably give you more sex in ten minutes than I can give you in ten days!"

The tears of anger were beginning to flood into her eyes and she got to her feet before he could see them. "So let's keep it business!" she said angrily. "See you at the starting line tomorrow!"

She turned and started out, almost knocking over Ileana who was on her way to the table. Ileana looked after her and then sat down in the seat she had vacated.

170

She looked at Cesare. "Who was that?" she asked curiously.

Cesare watched Luke go out the door. "My mechanic," he answered.

Ileana raised an eyebrow. "Oh?" She turned to the waiter who just came up. "Cinzano on the rocks, please." The waiter left. "Your mechanic," she repeated.

Cesare looked at her. "That's right!" he snapped.

Ileana smiled. "You know I could not help overhearing her last few remarks. She is right, you know."

Cesare didn't answer. The waiter placed her drink on the table and left. She picked up the drink and held it toward him in a sort of mock toast.

"Just the same, I do not think I will meet you in Cuernavaca as we had planned. I will wait right here for you in Mexico City," she said. She sipped her drink. "Not being American and therefore very understanding about such things, I think I shall give both of you the chance to find out for yourselves and prove each other right."

18

The bright sunlight hurt her eyes after the dimness of the cocktail lounge. She put on her dark glasses and began to walk. At first she walked quickly, angry with herself. Then she noticed people were looking at her strangely. She slowed down. After all this was Mexico City. And nobody down here walked fast.

What was there about her that brought on things like this? Even when she had been a kid, it had been like that. Other girls had fellows at their houses for a study session and nothing ever happened to them. She had played it as straight as they did but something would always happen before the evening was over.

When the boy had gone, she used to sit and curse herself. Usually she never saw the boy again but there was always another. And it would start the same way. She had the highest resolves. Just the schoolbooks.

She wouldn't even go near him, would sit on the other side of the table or across the room and they would throw each other questions. At least that was the way the evening would begin.

But before long she would feel the fever begin inside her. Her legs would grow weak and her speech begin to falter. She would find it more and more difficult to concentrate on the lessons. She would fight the fever inside her, fight so hard the perspiration would break out on her face and her arms so that even she would get the faint scent of musk that rose mixed with perfume from her body.

And then it would happen. The first few exploratory kisses. She would prove it to herself. Just those kisses and then she would stop. Nothing more after that. Then suddenly the fever would rise inside her and with it would come the frenzy. The frantic tearing of clothing that was constricting her, the wild desire to cause pain and to feel pain. The worship of the arrogant male and the need to subdue it inside her so she could be the master of its exploding strength.

She began to feel dizzy. Unconsciously she shook her head. She glanced up at the sun. It was still hot. Too hot. She had better go inside and sit down. She would feel better in the shade.

She looked around. She had walked almost back to the garage. That was good. She would go there and check the car again. There was something cold and masculine about a racing car that always made her feel better.

The garage felt cool after the heat outside. Most of the men had gone, it was near dinner time. She walked down the ramp.

STILETTO

Esteban came out of his little office and called after her. "Hola, Señorita Nichols!"

She turned toward him, smiling. "Hello, Señor Esteban."

He hurried up to her. "You have seen the Count?" he asked. "He is satisfied?"

She nodded. "I owe you many thanks, Señor Esteban."

"*No hay de que,*" he said. "I am glad to be of service to both of you." He looked up at her shrewdly. "An interesting man, this Count Cardinali, no?"

"*Si,*" she answered. "Very interesting. But tell me this, is he good?"

He looked at her. "He could be the best. But there is something missing."

They started to walk down the ramp. "Missing? I don't understand." She asked, "What is missing?"

"Fear," he answered. "A racer is like a matador. Neither are any good until they have tasted fear. Once they have done that, they develop their skill. They don't do foolish unnecessary things. They just drive to win."

They came to a stop in front of the long white Ferrari. "He doesn't care about winning?" she asked, walking over to the car and resting her hand on it.

"A beautiful automobile," he said.

She looked down at it. Unconsciously she rubbed her hand across the fender. "The best in the garage," she said.

He smiled shrewdly. "I think maybe this time I will bet my ten pesos on the Count." He started back up the ramp. "Good luck, señorita."

She watched him until he disappeared around the

175

turn. Then she opened the door and sat down in the car. The harsh mixed odor of oil and gasoline and the rubbed leather of the seat come up to her. She slid over behind the wheel and put her hands upon it. This was strength. Pure male strength.

She remembered sitting in her father's lap while he drove their car in to town to do their marketing. How big she had felt and how she had waved for everyone to see she was driving. Even Mr. Saunders, the fat policeman who directed traffic on Main Street, came over to see if she had a license. She was only six years old then.

She knew how to drive before she was ten years old. Papa used to let her run the car on the back road behind the house. Mother used to shake her head.

"Half the time she doesn't act like a girl at all," her mother used to say. "Always hanging around the garage, fooling with cars and hearing all kinds of talk from the roughneck boys that hang around there too."

"Aw, let her go, Ma," her father used to say tolerantly. "Time enough for her to grow up and learn to cook and sew. That ain't so important nowadays anyhow with everything coming in cans and frozen packages and dresses all readymade." He was secretly pleased. He always wanted a son.

It was better when she was sixteen and got her license to drive. Somehow the boys didn't bother her so much then. She didn't feel the need to tear them down so much. Maybe it was because she took it out on them on the road and in the drag races they used to hold out on the Ocean Drive.

She knew what they thought the first time she came up to them in her own hot rod. Here comes "Easy,"

176

looking to get laid. She knew the stories that went around the school about her. That whenever a boy showed up in the locker room with scratches on his back, the other boys would laugh and begin to pitch nickels at him. It didn't stop them from clustering around her car when she drove up though.

Johnny Jordan, the leader of the boys, had swaggered up to the car. He leaned over the door, a cigarette drooping from his lips. "Where'ja get the jalopy?" he asked.

"At Stan's," she said, mentioning the name of the garage where all the boys picked up their second-hand cars.

He looked it up and down critically. "I never seen it there," he said.

"I did a little work on it myself," she lied. It wasn't a little work. She had taken the car apart and rebuilt it by hand. It was a beat-up Pontiac convertible that had been in a wreck when she got it. She had taken out the motor and replaced it with a Cadillac engine, put in a new differential, repacked the bearings, widened the brake bands, cut down the body and fitted an old Cord frame over it, then poured lead into the doors to give it weight, and painted it shining silver and black. It had taken her six months.

"Does it go?" Johnny asked her.

"It goes," she said.

"Move over," he said, starting to get in.

She sat firmly behind the wheel. "Uh-uh," she said. "Nobody gets to drive this until I take a few."

He stared at her. "Who yuh gonna get to drag yuh? Ain't nobody here gonna race a girl."

She smiled. "Chicken?" she asked.

177

His face flushed. "Ain't that," he said. "Who ever heard of a girl ridin' drag? It just ain't done."

"Okay," she said. She started the motor again. "I'll tell 'em back in town that you're all afraid." She started to back down the road from them.

Johnny started after her. "Hey, wait a minute. You got no right to say that."

She stopped the car and smiled at him. "Oh, no? Then prove it."

"Okay," he said reluctantly. "But don't blame me if you get hurt."

He pulled his car up beside her. "Drag up the road one mile," he shouted over the noise of the engines. "Then you hold up there an' I'll come back and we'll go 'chicken.'"

She nodded and watched the starter. The boy dropped his hand. She released the clutch and the car jumped forward. She double-clutched into high and looked over at Johnny. His car was even with her. She laughed excitedly and swung toward him. They were no more than a few inches apart now.

He hit the accelerator trying to inch in front of her. She laughed again and opened up the throttle. He didn't gain an inch. She moved the car in closer toward him. There was the sound of metal on metal and he moved away to give her room. He was riding half on the shoulder of the road now. She stepped on the accelerator and went away from him as if he were standing still.

She had the car already turned around as he swung past her and went back down the road. He glared balefully at her as he went by.

STILETTO

She watched for the starter's signal again. When it came, she was ready and the car leaped down the road. Then they were coming at each other in the dead center of the pavement. She smiled and put her foot all the way down on the floor. The wheel was steady in her hands.

When she looked up, his car was almost upon her. Her smile became frozen on her face. She wouldn't turn the wheel. She wouldn't.

At the last possible moment she saw him turn his wheel. There was a flash of his white face, cursing as he passed. She watched his car in the mirror as she slowed down. It was swerving wildly but he brought it under control and came to a stop. She turned around and drove back to him.

He was out of his car and the boys were around him. They were staring at his left rear fender. It was half torn off. She didn't even know that she had hit the rear of his car as they passed.

He looked up at her. "You're crazy!" he said.

She smiled and slid over on the seat. "Want to drive?" she asked. "It can do a hundred and twenty on the stretch."

He walked around the car and got in beside her. He put the car into gear and they moved off. In a moment he had the car up to ninety miles per hour. He was her first steady.

It had been different with him. Not like the others. She felt easier, more sure of herself. They didn't have to go at it like cats and dogs. He respected her. He knew she was his equal. All the same it didn't keep him from making her pregnant.

179

She was in her last year in high school. She waited one week and then went to him. "We're gonna have to get married," she said.

"Why?" he asked her.

"Why do you think, stupid?" she snapped.

He stared at her then he cursed. "God damn!" he said. "It's those lousy cheap rubbers I bought at the drive-in!"

"It wasn't the rubbers that did it," she said. She began to get angry. "It was that goddam thing of yours. You never stopped poking it at me."

"You seemed to like it good enough," he said. "You never said no!" He glared at her. "Besides how do I know it's even mine? I heard enough stories about you!"

She stared at him for a moment and all the dreams she had had about the two of them came tumbling down. Deep inside him, he was just like all the others. She turned on her heels and walked away from him.

The next Saturday she drew a hundred dollars from her savings account and drove up to Center City. There was a doctor there in Mex town who had taken care of some of the girls at school.

Silently she waited until all the other patients had gone, then she walked into the office. He was a fat little man with a shining bald head. He looked tired.

"Take off your dress and come over here," he said.

She hung her dress on the wall hook and turned toward him.

"All your clothes," he said.

She took off her brassière and panties and walked over to him. He got up from behind his desk and came around it toward her. He felt her breasts and her

180

stomach and listened to her heart. He came up to about her shoulders. He led her over to a long narrow table. "Put your hands on the edge and bend way over," he said, putting a rubber finger on his right hand. "Take a deep breath and let it out slowly," he said.

She took a deep breath and let it slip past her open mouth while he did something inside her. Then he was finished and she straightened up and turned around.

He looked up into her face. "About six weeks I figure," he said.

She nodded. "That's about right."

He went back to his desk and sat down. "It'll be a hundred dollars," he said.

Silently she went over to her purse and took out the money. She counted it out on the desk before him.

"When do you want it done?" he asked.

"Right now," she said.

"You can't stay here," he said. "You got anyone with you?"

She shook her head. "I got my car outside." The doctor looked at her skeptically. "Don't worry about me," she said. "I'll get home all right."

He picked up the hundred dollars and put it in his desk. He walked over to the sterilizer and took out a hypodermic. He fitted it into a small bottle and approached her as he drew the liquid up into the syringe.

"What's that?" she asked, for the first time feeling a little fear.

"Penicillin." He smiled. "Thank God for it. It kills every bug there is except the one you got inside you."

He was deft and quick and competent. It was over in twenty minutes. He helped her down from the table and helped her dress. He gave her some pills in a small envelope that had no markings on it.

"The big ones are penicillin," he said. "Take one of them every four hours for the next two days. The small ones are pain killers. Take one of them every two hours after you get home. Get right into bed and stay there for at least two days. Don't worry if you bleed a lot, that's normal. If you feel you're losing too much blood after the first day, don't be a fool, call your doctor. If your mother asks any questions tell her you got a heavy curse. Remember all that?"

She nodded her head.

"All right, then," he said gently. "You can go. Get right home and into bed. In an hour you'll be in so much pain, you'll wish you'd never been born."

He went back to his desk and sat down as she went to the door. She turned and looked back at him. "Thank you, doctor," she said.

He looked up at her. "It's all right," he said. "But get smart now. I don't want to see you back here again."

She made the forty miles to her home in less than a half hour. She was beginning to feel lightheaded and weak when she stopped the car in front of her house. She went right upstairs to her room, grateful that the house was empty. She gulped one of each of the pills quickly and crept under the sheets, beginning to shiver with the pain.

About a week later, she was pulling her car out of the parking lot behind the supermarket when Johnny came over and put his hands on the door.

"I been thinkin', Luke," he said with that masculine sureness that was so irritating. "We kin get married."

"Drop dead, you chicken shit!" she said coldly and shot the car out of the lot, almost taking his arm off.

After that it was the car. By the time she entered college she had already achieved a certain amount of fame locally. Every week she entered the stock-car races at the Cow Pasture Track. She began to win with a regularity that made her a favorite with the townsfolk. They began to speak with pride of the little girl who drove even the professional drivers off the track.

It was during her first summer vacation that she got married. He was a racing-car driver of course. He was six-feet-three, with curly black hair and laughing brown eyes and the best driver at the meet. He came from West Texas and spoke with a drawl.

"I reckon you 'n' me ought to hook up, little one," he said, looking down at her. "Between the two of us we're the best on the road."

"You mean you want to marry me?" she asked, feeling the fever start up inside her again.

"I reckon so," he said. "That's what I mean."

Her parents were against it. They wanted her to finish school and become a teacher. There was plenty of time for her to get married. Besides, what kind of a life would she lead, traipsing all around the country to every cheap little auto track there was?

That was the wrong argument to use because that was exactly the kind of life she wanted to lead. It was only behind the wheel of a car that she really came alive. That made everything and everybody equal. And the strange thing about it was that they did pretty well at it too. Within a year she had managed to put almost fifteen thousand dollars in the bank.

Then the police came in and arrested her husband for bigamy. It seemed he had three wives before her that he had neglected to divorce. And two weeks after they took him off to jail, she discovered she was pregnant. This time she had the baby. It was a boy.

She took him home and left him with her parents. Then she bought a plane ticket to Europe and bought a Ferrari. In France she entered a race for women and won. The prize wasn't very much but now she had a Ferrari and two thousand dollars in the bank. And she was through with the cheap tracks. From now on it was nothing but the big ones.

It was in Monaco that she met the Irishman. He drove well and he laughed a lot. He had only one fault. He gambled. But the fever was inside her whenever she looked at him. This time she didn't marry him though she might just as well have. They went everywhere in the world together, drove madly in every country and he was always broke.

It was in Mexico just before the race last year that he came to her. For the first time she saw fear in his eyes. "It's the gamblers, me darlin'," he said. "They'll murder me if I don't pay them." He broke down and began to cry.

"How much?" she asked.

He looked up at her, hope rising in his eyes like a whipped puppy. "Ten thousand dollars," he said.

"I have four in the bank," she said. "I can get six on the car."

He had seized her hand and kissed it gratefully. "I'll pay you back," he swore. "Ivery penny of it."

184

The next day he came to the bank with her while she got the money. When she gave it to him, he said he would meet her back at the hotel for dinner. He never showed up. By ten o'clock that night the news was all over the garage. He had run away with the wife of another driver.

She lost the race and the bank took the car. She was sitting in the hotel room wondering how she was going to get the money to pay the bill when a knock came at the door.

She walked over and opened it. A neatly dressed man who had an oddly familiar-looking face stood there. "Miss Nichols?" he asked.

She nodded.

"May I come in?" he asked.

She stepped back. He came into the room and she closed the door. He turned to face her. "I have long been an admirer of yours," he said. "I have seen you race in many places. Italy, France, Monaco. I also have heard you have a little problem. I would like to help you."

She opened the door again. "Get out," she said.

He held up his hand, smiling. "Don't be so quick. It's nothing like that. You drive racing cars. I own one. I want you to drive it for me."

She closed the door. "Where is it?"

"In Acapulco," he answered. "The race is from there into California. I will settle up all your bills here and give you one thousand dollars when you deliver the car to the garage at the end of the race. You may keep whatever purse you win."

"What's the catch?" she asked. "The car weighted down with dope?"

He smiled again. "All you have to do is drive the car. For that you will get paid." He took out a thin Italian cigar and lit it. "You don't have to know anything more than that."

She stared at him. It was either take his offer or wire her parents for the money. It wasn't that they would refuse her but if she took their money she would have to return home. She would never get the chance to get another car then, she would never have enough money. She would be stuck there.

"I'll do it," she said.

"Good." He smiled. "There will be a money order at the desk when you come downstairs in the morning." He gave her a few more instructions and then left before she had a chance to ask him his name.

It wasn't until she was aboard the plane the next day that it came to her. She had seen him in Rome at a restaurant. Someone had pointed him out.

"That's Emilio Matteo," he had said. "One of the three most important men in the Mafia today. The U.S. kicked him out but it hasn't seemed to stop him very much. He gets around all right."

Six times more during the next year she saw him. Each time it was to perform some errand for him. She had to be a fool not to know that she had become a messenger for the Mafia. And she was not a fool.

But each time there was another thousand dollars in the bank. There was eight thousand there now. Five more and she could get that Ferrari.

By this time she and Matteo were practically old friends. And she had read enough in the newspapers to know she was leading a man to his death. Not that it made any great difference to her. She had seen too many men die in the races. In tortured turning, twisting, burning wrecks. Everybody had to die sometime. That was the chance you took when you got behind the wheel.

At least that was the way she had felt before she met him. Before she felt the fever burning in her loins, the weakness in her legs. Before she felt the fire leap between them at his touch.

19

Cesare had just finished dressing when she came into his room. He looked up in surprise. "Ileana! What are you doing up at six o'clock in the morning?"

She finished tying the robe around her. "I couldn't let you go without wishing you good luck in the race."

He flashed a quick smile at her and bent to snap his boots. "That's very kind of you. Thank you." He straightened up and came over and kissed her cheek, then started for the door.

At the door he turned and looked back at her. "See you at dinner tonight," he said automatically.

"Dinner, tonight?" Her voice was puzzled. "I thought the race was going to take two or three days."

An annoyed look came to his face. "That's right, I forgot," he said quickly, realizing his inadvertent slip. He forced a smile to his lips. "It is becoming a habit to see you every evening."

STILETTO

A vague sense of warning began ticking in her mind. Cesare wasn't the kind of man who made mistakes like that. "Good or bad habit?" she asked.

He grinned. "You tell me when I get back," he said, closing the door behind him.

She stood there for a moment then turned back to the bedroom. His valise lay open on the bed. Idly she went over and began to close it. A flap fell forward from the top of the case. She bent to straighten it before she closed the lid.

It was a peculiar triangle-shaped flap that took up a small diagonal corner of the valise. Inside it was a thin stitched sheath that was fastened to the flap. It had recently held a knife. She could tell that from the stretched appearance.

A picture of the stiletto that Cesare held in his hand the night he found her in his apartment flashed through her mind. Why would he need a knife like that in an automobile race?

The vague sense of warning that had troubled her when he had said he would see her at dinner came back. Maybe it was the truth even if he said it was a mistake afterward. Maybe those men were right in what they had said, even though she did not believe them at the time.

A feeling of panic began to rise inside her. Suddenly she knew why he had taken the knife. He was coming back tonight to kill her.

Luke looked across the car at Cesare. He was driving easily, his eyes hidden beneath the large black goggles, a faint smile on his lips. She leaned forward to check the dash.

STILETTO

The tach needle stood at 26,000 r.p.m., it checked out with speedometer. The temperature gauge was normal, the oil pressure gauge was even, the generator and the battery were at normal discharge. She straightened up. They could go a million miles in this car if they wanted to.

They turned the corner and came upon two other contestants. Cesare looked at her. "Can we have a little fun before we quit?" he shouted over the motor.

She glanced at the mileage indicator. They were about sixty miles from the starting point. She nodded.

Cesare grinned and hit the accelerator. He cut in behind the two cars. They were blocking his way through. He inched up until he was practically riding their rear bumpers.

She looked at him. His lips were drawn back across his teeth in a savage grin. Beneath the goggles his eyes seemed to shine with an unholy joy. The cars in front of him began to go into a curve.

He laughed aloud and picked up more speed. She looked down at the speedometer. They were doing one hundred and twenty now and the needle was climbing. She felt the drag on her body as the big Ferrari tore into the curve. She looked ahead nervously. If the cars in front didn't split now, they would all be dead. Before the thought had gone from her mind, the Ferarri had crept between the two cars. They had split.

Deliberately, Cesare sawed the Ferrari back and forth across the road. She could see the other drivers cursing and fighting to stay on the road. Then they came into the straightaway and now the Ferrari was a few feet ahead of them. Cesare laughed aloud again and opened the car up. The speedometer jumped to one-fifty and the Ferrari left the two cars behind them.

She looked back at them and laughed. Now she knew what Esteban had meant back in the garage. Here was a race that Cardinali knew he wasn't even going to finish and still he drove the same way he always did. But he could drive. Esteban was right. If he really wanted to he could be the best in the business.

She felt his hand come down on her own and she turned around. Unconsciously, she had moved closer to him in the excitement. He lifted her hand from the seat and moved it on to his thigh. She looked up at him. He turned his head and met her gaze, a mocking smile on his lips.

She could feel the heat coming up from his leg into her hand and running into her body. For a moment she was wild at what he could do to her, how he could make her feel. She dug her fingers into the muscles of his thigh, feeling her nails go through his clothing into his flesh. She wanted him to feel pain, to hurt and push her hand away.

He only laughed aloud at her. She felt a pulse begin to throb in the palm of her hand. Angrily she raked her nails back along his leg and took away her hand. She moved away from him. She closed her eyes at the sudden pain that came up inside her when she lost contact with his warmth. She shook her head to clear it. What was the matter with her anyway? There was no percentage in it. Did she always have to try to be a loser?

She looked down at the mileage indicator. They were a hundred miles from the starting point. She tapped him on the shoulder. "Begin slowing down. We better let those cars behind us go by."

Cesare nodded. The big Ferrari began to lose speed. They were down to sixty miles per hour and it felt as if they were standing still. Within a few minutes the two cars they had passed went by with much hooting of their horns.

He shook his head. "The party's over," he said.

"It never really began," she replied, her eye on the mileage indicator.

The one-fifteen was creeping up on the dial. He seemed to be paying no attention to it. She looked at him. Sixty miles an hour was still too fast to be going if even a small bomb was going to blow up your generator but if he thought she was going to chicken, he was crazy.

The one-fifteen locked in the dial. He laughed and hit the accelerator. The big car began to leap forward. At the same moment, there was a faint explosion under the hood. The car shuddered and the motor stopped. They began to weave crazily on the road.

She could see the muscles on his forearms ridge as he fought to hold the wheel steady while he pumped the brake a little at a time to bring the speed down. At last they were rolling slowly. She let her breath out slowly. "Now that you've had your fun, Mr. Cardinali," she said sarcastically, "I guess it's safe to pull off the road now."

"Okay," he said. He turned the wheel toward the shoulder of the road. He smiled at her.

"Look out!" she yelled, seeing it first. "A ditch!"

Cesare spun the wheel sharply but it was too late.

The two wheels on the right side of the car caught the ditch. Slowly the heavy car settled in the sandy earth and rolled over on its top.

Cesare slid out from under the car. He got to his feet and pulled off his helmet. Faint wisps of smoke began to come up from the engine. He turned back to the car. "Luke! Are you all right?"

Her voice came faintly from beneath the other side of the car. "I'm okay."

He ran around the car and knelt beside it. He peered under the car. She had her hands on the back of the seat and was squirming around, trying to get out.

"What are you waiting for?" he yelled. "Come on out. There are fifty gallons of gasoline back in the tank!"

She stopped squirming and stared at him balefully. "What the hell do you think I'm trying to do? A snake dance?" she snapped, beginning to wriggle again. Suddenly she began to laugh. "My coveralls are caught on something."

He threw himself to the ground beneath her. "Why didn't you say so?" he grinned. He put his hands under the coveralls and ripped them open. Then she felt his arms under her shoulders. "Kick your shoes off," he commanded.

Automatically she did as he told her. She felt herself slide forward, out of the coveralls onto the ground beside him. She was still laughing.

He looked at her, a faint smile beginning to twitch the corners of his mouth. "Well, you said it was safe."

"Show-off!" she retorted.

"Who is showing off now?" he asked, his eyes glancing down at her.

STILETTO

The laughter faded from her lips. She was suddenly aware of her near nudity. The thin brassière and panties didn't serve to cover very much. "I'll get my coveralls," she said, turning to reach for them.

His hand fell on her shoulder, pinning her to the ground. She lay there motionless feeling the warmth in his hand, staring up at him. She felt his other hand move and free one breast from her brassière. She looked down at herself then back up at him, oddly aroused at the sight of her white flesh against his darkly tanned hand.

"Stop it," she said in a low voice, the fever beginning to work inside her. This time she wasn't going to be easy.

His eyes were glowing. She felt as if she were under a microscope, as if he could read every hidden thought, knew every emotion inside her. "You don't want me to stop," he said.

She felt his strong fingers suddenly crush her breast and the pain tore her from her lethargy. "I'll make you stop!" she screamed, thrusting her hands inside his open shirt, her body writhing wildly. "I'll tear your flesh into ribbons!"

But when her fingers felt the soft cool touch of his skin, the fever rose and took possession of her body and the strength drained from her limbs. She thrust her hands deeper into his shirt and closed her eyes. His arm held her away.

She opened her eyes, feeling the tears come to them. It was no use. She couldn't change, she would never change. "Let me touch you, let me worship you," she begged.

And when, after a while, he took her, she knew she

195

had been right from the moment she first saw him. Never had there been a man like him before that could fit and fill every hidden corner of her mind and body.

She closed her eyes and began to run softly through the forest toward the mountain. She knew the animal was there somewhere, his black and yellow stripes, stalking her in the brush. She was scrambling frantically up the mountain now, her heart pounding, her breath like a rasping fire inside her lungs. Then she was on the peak with the whole world spinning round below her, this time when the animal sprang she was ready for him. Locked in an embrace of death, they tumbled together, over and over down the face of the mountain.

She moaned softly. "Tiger, tiger tiger!"

Cesare kicked open the door of the shack. "There is no one here," he said.

She walked into the shack and he followed her. "What do we do now?" he asked.

"We wait," she said succinctly.

There were a few battered chairs and a table in the shack. He pulled one of the chairs toward her. She sat down. He lit two cigarettes and held one toward her. She took it without speaking.

"You are very silent," he said.

She blew the smoke from her lungs, its acrid taste somehow cleansing. "What is there to say?" she asked. "You made your point."

"Was that all there was to it?" he asked.

She stared at him. "What difference does it make? It won't happen again."

196

"Are you always that sure of everything? How do you know what will happen tomorrow?"

"Tomorrow I'll have enough money to buy a Ferrari," she said almost bitterly. "And we'll never see each other again."

"Is that all it meant to you?" He laughed shortly. "An automobile? A Ferrari can do many things but it cannot love you."

"You speak of love?" she said cynically. "You forget I know about you. To how many women have you spoken of love? Ten, twenty, a hundred? More?"

His eyes were veiled. "A man may live in many places and still not call them home."

The sound of an automobile came from outside the shack. Luke got up from her chair and walked past him to the door. She turned and looked back at him. Her face was set and tense. "It's over," she said with finality. "I said I was never going to be a loser again."

"You changed your mind back there, under the automobile," he said softly.

"I was paid for what I did," she said harshly. "I was told to keep you here." She swung open the door.

Two men stood there, the guns in their hands pointed at Cesare.

She looked back at him over her shoulder. "See what I mean?" she asked, stepping carefully behind them and out into the sunlight. "We did not come to praise Cesare," she said.

20

The door closed behind them, cutting off the sunlight. They stood there, staring at Cesare.

"Where's Matteo?" he asked.

Allie smiled. "He couldn't come. He sent us."

Cesare felt his muscles tense. His lips were suddenly dry. He wet them with his tongue. It didn't make sense to him. Any of it. Matteo had nothing to gain by his death. None of them. "It must be a mistake," he said.

Allie shook his head. "It's no mistake." He stepped forward, motioning with the gun. "Turn around and face the wall and put your hands on it. Over your head. Real slow."

Cesare looked at him, then slowly did as he was told. He felt Allie's hand check him down. "There is no gun," he said.

"I ain't lookin' for a gun," Allie said quickly.

The stiletto felt cold against Cesare's arm over his head. "You won't find the knife either," he said. "I don't need it to drive a car."

Allie stepped back. "I guess not," he admitted. "Well, you won't need it any more."

The gunman looked at him. "Hit him now, Allie?" He began to raise his gun.

Allie stopped him with a gesture. "No. I got my own plans. This guy gets something special."

Cesare looked back over his shoulder. Allie was taking something out of his pocket. He saw Cesare watching him and grinned. "Know what this is, baby?" he asked, holding it in the air.

Cesare didn't answer. He knew.

"It's an ice pick," Allie was still grinning. "It ain't got a fancy name like that pig sticker you use but it does a job. Big Dutch could have told you that." Quickly he reversed the gun in his hand and swiped it viciously across the back of Cesare's head.

His mind reeling, Cesare went to his knees, his fingers trying to hold onto the wall. He heard Allie's harsh voice.

"Turn around, ya' bastard! I want ya' to see what's comin'!"

Slowly he turned around. He shook his head, his vision beginning to clear. He stared up at Allie.

Allie was smiling. He dropped the gun into his pocket and transferred the ice pick to his right hand. He put his face very close to Cesare. "Yuh're gonna get this right in the gizzard!" he snarled.

Cesare watched him raise the ice pick. He threw himself desperately to the side as the ice pick came slashing down. The pick went into the rotten wood of the wall behind him and stuck there. He swung his hand in a vicious judo chop at Allie's throat.

Without waiting the result of the blow he flung himself across the room at the gunman. The gun flew from the man's hand as they sprawled to the floor. From the corner of his eye, Cesare saw Allie pick up the gun. He rolled over, clasping the gunman to him as a shield, just as Allie began to fire.

The man's body jerked with the impact of the bullets. He squirmed for a moment, trying to loosen himself then went limp in Cesare's grasp. He began to fall to the floor and Cesare tried to scramble for the door.

Allie laughed. "No, ya' don't, ya' bastard!" He squeezed the trigger.

There was a click as the hammer fell on an empty chamber. He swore and threw the gun at Cesare. He turned, grabbing for the ice pick. He pulled it from the wall and turned just in time to see Cesare moving toward him slowly, the stiletto gleaming in his hand.

He held the ice pick out in front of him as he began to move along the wall. He remembered the gun he had dropped into his pocket. A smile began to come to his lips as he surreptitiously dropped his hand to get it. All he needed was a moment of time.

She sat in the front seat of the car behind the wheel absolutely motionless. Her hands gripped the wheel so hard that her knuckles were white and her eyes were focused on some distant point in space beyond the windshield. It wasn't until she felt the point of the stiletto touch her throat that she turned her head and saw him.

He leaned toward her, his lips drawn back in an animal-like snarl across his tense face. His blue eyes shone with a yellow light in the sun.

Her eyes widened for a moment with an expression he did not understand, then went blank and guarded. She did not speak.

"Why did you do it?" he asked, the stiletto steady in his hand.

She looked up at him. Her voice was as empty as her eyes. "I told you before. It was my job. I didn't ask questions of Matteo. Did you?"

The yellow light seemed to flame up in his eyes. "That was different. I kept my oath."

"And so did I," she said. "The only difference was in the manner in which we were paid for what we did."

"I ought to kill you!" he said harshly.

She felt the point of the stiletto press against her throat. She closed her eyes and leaned her head back against the top of the seat. "Go ahead," she said wearily. "It really doesn't matter. Matteo will not tolerate my failure any more than he did your success."

He did not speak and the silence that followed seemed interminable. She felt the fever rise suddenly within her, radiating through her body like a shock wave of heat. The image of the tiger leaped into her mind. In another moment, she would not be able to control the auto-orgiastic convulsions that were already taking possession of her loins. "Go ahead! Get it over with!" she cried wildly. Death would still the tiger too.

Again he did not answer and she opened her eyes. His face was bathed in perspiration and she could feel the trembling of his body against the seat. A sudden recognition came to her and she saw herself deep inside him. "Oh, God!" she cried faintly, reaching up to him. They were so alike.

She heard the stiletto drop to the floor of the car as she felt his lips seek her throat and cover the tiny bleeding wound left there by the knife. The danger and the excitement were over and they were the same for him as they were for her. They only served to whet the appetite of the tiger.

He stopped the car in front of her hotel. "Get your things and meet me at the airport in two hours," he said.

"You will be careful?" she asked, looking at him.

He nodded confidently. "We will be on our way back to New York before anyone knows what happened. Somehow I must get in touch with Emilio. He will straighten this out."

She pressed his hand and got out of the car. She watched him drive off and then went into her hotel.

He walked into the lobby of El Ciudad and over to the desk. "My key, please," he asked of the clerk who had his back toward him.

The clerk turned around. "Count Cardinali!" he exclaimed, a note of surprise in his voice. He reached for the key behind him and placed it on the desk. "The race—"

Cesare interrupted him. "My generator burned out."

"I am sorry, señor," the clerk said. He brought up an envelope and gave it to Cesare. "The Baroness left this for you."

203

Cesare opened the note. It was in Ileana's hand-writing.

"Sorry, Darling, I could not wait for your return. Have left for New York with a rich Texan who insists that we do some holiday shopping. Love, Ileana."

Cesare smiled to himself. He should have known that Ileana had a reason not to meet him in Cuernavaca. He looked up at the clerk. "What time did the Baroness leave?" he asked.

"About eleven o'clock this morning," the clerk replied with a knowing smirk.

Cesare nodded and started toward the elevator. He checked his watch. It was about seven o'clock. Ileana was probably in New York already.

21

Baker leaned across his desk and stared at Ileana. "Why did you come back? You were supposed to stay with him."

"I was afraid, I told you." Ileana looked at him nervously. "I had a feeling that he was going to kill me. That he knew . . ."

"What made you feel like that?" Baker asked quickly. "Was it something he said or did? Something you saw?"

Ileana shook her head. "It was nothing like that. It was just that flap on the suitcase that I told you about. When I touched it I had the feeling that death had taken possession of his soul. So I came back."

"But you never saw a stiletto there," Baker said. "I have a flap like that in my valise. It's for my toothbrush holder and razor." There was a knock at the door. "Come in," he called.

An agent entered, carrying a teletype. He put it on Baker's desk. "This just came in from Mexico City," he said. "They found the bodies of Allie Fargo and some hood in a deserted hut on the desert about a half mile from where Cardinali's car went off the road."

Ileana rose excitedly. "See! I was right!"

Baker looked up at her. "Maybe if you had stayed, we would know more about this."

"Maybe, also, I would be dead!" Ileana snapped. "I don't like this at all."

Baker looked up at the agent. "Where is Cardinali now?" he asked.

"On his way back to New York. His plane is due at Idlewild in the morning," the agent replied. "He has a woman with him."

Baker turned back to Ileana. "A woman?" he asked. "Is that why you came back?"

"Don't be silly!" Ileana snapped.

Baker began to smile. "I'm beginning to get the picture. He found another girl friend and told you to beat it."

Ileana rose to the bait. "That's not true," she retorted. "I know the girl. She's his mechanic."

"His mechanic?" Baker said skeptically.

She nodded. "Her name is Luke something. His regular mechanic was ill and he hired her down there."

Baker turned back to the agent. "Wire down there and get me the rundown on her."

"Yes, sir," the agent said. "Do you want Cardinali picked up when the plane lands?"

Baker shook his head. "That won't do any good. We

have nothing to hold him on. Just have a car ready for me. I want to see where he goes when he lands."

The agent left the room and Baker looked across the desk at Ileana. "You better go back to the hotel and stay as close to him as you can."

"I will not!" Ileana said quickly.

"He won't harm you as long as he doesn't know about us." His voice hardened. "Or would you prefer deportation?"

"Being deported is better than being dead," she retorted.

"Moral turpitude is a pretty serious charge," he continued. "It means you will never be able to enter this country again. And it doesn't look pretty in the newspapers."

She stared at him resentfully. "In Europe they are much more understanding. They realize some women are not made for work." She took out a cigarette and tapped it nervously on the desk.

Baker lit it for her and leaned back. He knew he had her now. "I think we Americans know that too." He smiled. "It's just that we don't talk about it."

She drew deeply on her cigarette. "I am beginning to get the impression that sex is considered un-American!"

He stared at her for a moment then he leaned across the desk. When he spoke his voice was almost gentle. "You're frightened, aren't you?"

She looked up into his eyes, then she nodded slowly. "At first I thought it was all a big joke. But now I realize it is not. I am beginning to get very frightened."

He got to his feet and walked around the desk to

207

her. "Try not to, Baroness," he said slowly. "We'll keep an eye on you. And I promise we'll get you out of there at the first sign of trouble."

The young agent with Baker whistled as he saw Luke get into the taxi with Cesare in front of the airport. "Say, that guy does pretty good with the dames, doesn't he, chief?"

Baker nodded. He watched the cab pull off. "Better get started," he said.

The agent pulled the car out into traffic. Another car cut in front of them. He looked over at Baker. "Want me to jump in front of him?"

Baker shook his head. "No, it's all right. Stay where you are. We can't lose him on the expressway."

They rode along silently for about ten minutes until they had almost reached the curve at Jamaica Bay. Baker looked at the car in front of them curiously. It still kept its position between their car and Cesare's taxi. Now it began to pick up speed and swung into the left lane. A feeling that something was going wrong began to come over him.

He had been in this business too long to disregard hunches. He opened his coat and loosened the revolver in its holster. "Stay with that car," he told the younger man. "I don't like it."

Obediently the agent swung into the left lane. "That car is acting peculiar," he said. A sound of muffled explosions came back to them. "They're shooting at him!" he shouted.

"Hit the gas!" Baker yelled back at him, whipping out his gun. He leaned out the window and fired at the car in front of them.

208

STILETTO

Cesare's taxi was going off the road on to the shoulder of grass as they sped past it. Baker couldn't tell whether anybody in it had been hurt. He fired his gun again.

A bullet hole appeared in the back window of the car directly behind the driver. The driver pitched forward across the wheel and the car plunged wildly off the road toward the bay. Just before it hit the water, Baker saw the door open and the man come tumbling out.

They were on the grass now and coming to a stop. Baker leaped from the car and took off after the running man. "Stop!" he shouted, firing a warning shot in the air.

The man turned for a moment. Baker saw something glint in his hand. There was a ping as the bullet went by him, then the sound of the shot.

Baker flung himself to the ground. The man was running again. Baker aimed low, for the man's legs. He squeezed the trigger gently. He wanted this one alive, to talk. His first shot missed. He fired again.

This time the man tumbled headlong to the ground. He rolled over and over and down a slight crest of the ground.

The young agent came running up, his gun in his hand. He looked down at Baker. "You okay?"

Baker began to get to his feet. "I'm okay."

"The one in the car is dead," the agent said.

Baker looked at him. "Go and look at the one over there. I tried to hit him in the legs."

The agent ran off and bent over the fallen man. "This one's dead too!" he yelled back.

Grimly Baker began to place his gun back in the holster. Cesare's voice came from behind him.

"You're a good shot, Mr. Baker." He was smiling.

Baker stared at him almost balefully. The man must have nerves of ice. He had just been shot at, two men had been killed and his voice was as calm as the day they met in his office. "You can't tell me they weren't shooting at you this time, Mr. Cardinali," he said, trying to keep his voice as calm as the other's.

Cesare shrugged his shoulders. "No, I can't, Mr. Baker." A kind of mocking challenge crept into his eyes. "What I don't understand is—why?"

Baker's eyes grew cold. He felt the pretenses slip away from him now. "And I suppose you don't know why Allie Fargo was killed in a shack not a half mile from where your car went off the road in Mexico either?"

Cesare smiled. "I did not even know that he had been killed. You see I did not read the newspapers."

"You can account for your time on the road?" Baker asked.

"Of course I can," Cesare said. "I was with my mechanic every moment. You can check with her. She is still in the taxi, repairing her makeup."

"You're pretty good at coming up with women to alibi you," Baker said sarcastically.

Cesare was still smiling. "Most fortunate," he agreed.

Baker stared at him for a moment as a police car came speeding up. "Go ahead, Cardinali, have your fun," he said angrily. "Just remember, we won't be around all the time to protect you!"

The cab pulled over to the curb and Cesare got

out. He leaned back into the cab. "Wait here," he said to Luke. "I have to run up to the office for a moment."

The receptionist seemed surprised to see him. He went by her into the general office. There was a group of employees standing around the water cooler. They looked up as he approached and scattered to their desks. He nodded to them and went into his office.

"Come inside," he said as he walked through Miss Martin's anteroom.

Inside his own office, he turned to her. "What's going on out there? Why aren't they working?" he demanded.

Miss Martin looked at him. "Are you all right?" she asked.

"Of course, I'm all right," he snapped.

"We just heard over the radio that somebody took some shots at you on the way into the city," she said.

"What excuse is that for them to be standing around doing nothing?" he asked angrily. "They are being paid to do their jobs, not to gossip."

"There is nothing for them to do," Miss Martin said.

"What do you mean, nothing?" He was getting angrier. "Why not?"

She picked up a telegram lying on his desk and gave it to him. "Our franchises have been revoked. That's the last one. It just came in about an hour ago."

He looked down at it and then picked up the other telegrams from his desk. They all read practically the same. The two Italian companies, the two English companies, the French company and the Swedish company. He looked up at her. "When did this happen?" he asked.

"It began the morning you left for Mexico," she said. "I don't understand it. It was almost as if someone gave the signal."

He looked down at the telegrams in his hand again. Angrily he threw them back on the desk. The Society was so sure of itself. So sure he would be dead that they didn't need to continue the franchises with his company. He would have to reach Matteo now. This business had gone far enough.

"I'm sorry, Mr. Cardinali," Miss Martin said sympathetically. "I tried to reach you but you had already left the hotel for the race. I guess it was because of all that business in the newspapers."

He didn't answer. He was thinking. Someone would have to get a message to the postmaster in his village in Sicily. He was sure that Matteo was in the country somewhere but he could spend the next twenty years and not find him. His secretary's voice cut into his thoughts.

"What are you going to do?" she asked.

He stared at her. "What else is there to do?" He shrugged. "Give everybody their severance pay and lay them off. Tell them we'll call them back as soon as the situation clears up."

"Do you think it will?" she asked.

"I don't know," he said, starting for the door. He stopped and looked back at her. "And, frankly, I don't give a damn!"

22

Cesare turned the key in the lock. He swung open the door. "Go on in," he said to Luke.

She walked into the apartment and he followed her, closing the door behind him. Ileana's voice came from the bedroom.

"Is that you, Cesare?"

He looked at Luke for a moment. Her face was expressionless. Then he smiled. "Yes, Ileana," he called.

Her voice still came from the bedroom. "I don't know what this world is coming to! All the rich Texans I meet are either married or phonies! This one actually wanted me to help him shop for his wife!"

He couldn't keep his smile from growing broader as the expression on Luke's face became more fixed. "That's too bad, Ileana," he said.

"I can't hear you," she replied. "But no matter.

213

I've had Tonio ice up some champagne for us. It's on the liquor cabinet. Be a dear, will you, and pour some for me. I'll be out in a minute!"

He walked over to the liquor cabinet. The champagne was there in an ice bucket with two glasses. Solemnly he took down another glass and stood it next to the others. Then he opened the bottle and began to pour the wine.

Ileana came to the doorway, tying the belt of her negligee. She was smiling. "I couldn't wait for you—" Her smile faded as she saw Luke standing in the center of the room. She cast a questioning glance at Cesare.

He looked from one to the other, enjoying the situation. "I believe you ladies have only met *en passant*." He smiled. "Allow me to introduce you."

He performed the introduction and gave each of them a glass of wine. He raised his glass in a toast. "To a happy friendship." He smiled and drank.

Ileana looked at Luke coldly then she turned to Cesare, smiling sweetly. "Though she is a little thin, don't you think your apartment is still too small for a *menage à trois?*" she asked in French.

Cesare answered in the same language. "Don't be a cat, Ileana. She has unsuspected talents."

"I don't doubt it," Ileana said dryly. "But if the hotel management objects to one, how do you think they will feel about two? Or have you told them you've turned Moslem?"

It was then the idea came to Cesare. He knew how to contact Matteo. The smile broadened on his lips. "It does not matter to them at all," he continued in French. "You see I have already told them you are leaving for Italy tonight and that she will occupy your room until you return!"

Ileana stared at him. "I will not do it!" she said angrily, still in French. "I will not step aside while you roll in the hay with that *chienne!*" She flung the glass at him and went back into the bedroom, slamming the door behind her.

The glass smashed against the cabinet and shattered into tiny fragments. Cesare looked down at them, then up at Luke. "Ileana has a rather quick temper," he said in English.

"The important thing is, will she go?" Luke asked in perfect French.

He stared at her for a moment, then began to laugh. "You understood?"

She was smiling now. "Every word." She nodded. "But that doesn't answer my question." The smile faded from her lips. "Will she go?"

"Of course she will," Cesare said confidently, still smiling. "Ileana and I are old friends. She will do anything for me."

Tonio put down the telephone and went back into the dining room. They looked up at him. "It was the airlines, Excellency," he said to Cesare. "They confirmed the Baroness' reservation for tonight!"

"Thank you, Tonio," Cesare said.

Ileana waited until Tonio had gone, then she turned to Cesare. "I won't do it!" she said angrily. "I don't care what you say. I won't do it!"

Cesare stared at her. Out of the corner of his eye he could see Luke looking at him with a knowing expression. He began to get angry. "You will do as I say, Ileana!" he said, his voice going hard. "Or would you like the immigration authorities to learn that you do not really work for me?"

Ileana looked over at Luke. Luke kept her eyes down on her plate. "Why don't you send her?" Ileana asked resentfully.

"You know I can't," Cesare snapped. "She would stick out like a sore thumb. Now, finish eating and pack your things. The jet to Rome leaves at midnight."

Angrily Ileana threw down her spoon and stormed from the table. They heard the door slam angrily behind her.

Luke looked up from her plate. There was a faint smile on her lips. "Ileana will do anything for me," she mimicked sarcastically.

Cesare stared at her, scowling. "Shut up!" he snapped angrily. "She's going, isn't she?"

Ileana came into her room and locked the door behind her. She crossed the room quickly and picked up the telephone and gave the operator a number. A voice answered. "Mr. Baker, please," she said.

He came on to the phone. "Yes?"

"He is sending me to Sicily, Mr. Baker," she said quickly in a low voice. "To his village. I'm to see the postmaster there and give him a message."

Baker's voice picked up interest. "What message?" he asked.

"It is this," Ileana said quoting. " 'Tell my uncle that I must meet with him.' Then I'm to wait in the

216

hotel until the postmaster gives me an answer to bring back to him."

"Good," Baker said. "Now we're beginning to get somewhere."

Ileana could feel the fear rising inside her. "Good. Is that all you have to say, Mr. Baker? Maybe you don't know it but Cesare's uncle has been dead for almost twelve years! One does not carry messages to and from a dead man!"

"Don't worry," he said soothingly. "The uncle you are taking a message to is very much alive. In the Society each man's sponsor is addressed by him as 'Uncle.'"

Her voice was suddenly very low. "If it is the Mafia I'm carrying a message to, Mr. Baker, then I am really frightened. They would not hesitate to kill me!"

"I told you before not to worry," he said still soothingly. "There will be a man on the plane with you and every place you go. You will never be alone. You did say you preferred rich Texans, didn't you? Well, look for the one on the plane with you."

Slowly she put down the telephone and lit a cigarette. She walked over to the french doors, opened them and walked out on the terrace in spite of the cold. She looked down at the city, its lights sparkling coldly in the winter night.

The sound of voices came floating up to her. Curiously, she looked over the parapet and down. The voices didn't come from the street but from the floor below her. Her balcony was set back from the one below. There was a young man and a girl in a close embrace down there.

In the night she could see the girl's white face turn upward in a kiss. They seemed oblivious to the cold. She shivered slightly and started back inside. She closed the doors carefully behind her.

It had been a long time since she had felt like the girl down there. Vaguely she wondered · if she ever would feel like that again. Suddenly she knew she never could. That was behind her, left in her mother's bedroom when she was nineteen years old.

For the first time in a long time she thought of her parents. Poor Daddy was lost. And Dearest, her mother, in her own way was lost. Strange that it should take so long for her to understand them.

It was only now, with no one to cling to and no one to love, that she could feel close to them. And lost like them. She felt the tears come welling up into her eyes. And cry for them.

23

Baker leaned across his desk and looked at Captain Strang. "Dan, I think we're getting our first break. Cardinali is asking his uncle for a meeting. If that meeting comes off and his uncle is who I think he is, we'll take the roof off this case!"

The policeman smiled. "It's about time. But what if the mob gets to Cardinali first?"

Baker nodded thoughtfully. "We can't let that happen. The stakes are too big."

"You can't be behind him every time they start shooting," Strang said quickly.

"I know," Baker said. "But I've got a plan."

"Let's hear it," Strang said.

Baker looked up at him, he lowered his voice to a confidential tone. "This will have to be between us. The chief won't like it. It's not regulation."

Strang smiled again. "I'm beginning to like it already," he said. "And I haven't even heard it yet."

"We'll frighten him into hiding," Baker said. "We'll start a campaign. Telephone calls every hour. Threats. We'll put the toughest looking guys on his tail and let him spot them. He'll think it's the mob. He's got to break. If only to hide until the meeting is set."

Strang looked at him thoughtfully. "It might work."

"It's got to work!" Baker said. "Once we've got him pinned down, then we can set up a stake-out that will work both ways. Nobody gets out, nobody gets in without our knowledge."

Strang stared at him. "It means our jobs if we louse it up."

Baker nodded. "I know."

"You got it real bad for that guy," Strang said.

"Real bad," Baker admitted. Emotion flooded through him so strongly that he rose from his chair and walked over to the window. When he spoke again, his voice was trembling. "I can understand most of these guys. I've seen the places they came from, the nothing they started out with. I know why they went wrong and how. But this one I don't get at all.

"He started out with everything. As far as we can see, he doesn't want anything. Maybe he's doing it just for kicks, maybe he likes to kill. I don't know.

"I only know if we don't find a way to stop him, a lot more people will die. And I don't mean only gangsters but innocent people like that girl in Florida. No one can tell where a psychopath like him will draw the line!"

Strang drew in his breath slowly. He took out his

pipe and knocked it against the ash tray. He stuck the empty pipe in his mouth and looked up at Baker. The smile in his eyes belied the grimness in his voice. "I've already put in thirty years with the force," he said. "And I never really wanted a steady job!"

The telephone began to ring. Cesare walked over and picked it up. "Cardinali speaking," he said into it.

The voice was rough and harsh and one he had never heard before "Cardinali?" the voice said menacingly. "The Stiletto has outlived its usefulness. We will get you sooner or later. Why don't you make it easy on yourself?"

The phone went dead in his hand. Impatiently Cesare jiggled the button. "Hello. Who is this? Who is this?"

There was no answer. He put down the receiver and walked back to the couch where Luke was sitting. She looked up at him curiously. "What was it?" she asked.

"A warning," he answered. "Probably from some cheap gangster."

Luke nodded thoughtfully. "That's how they begin. I've seen the pattern before. They'll try to wear you out."

Cesare was angry. "If they think they can panic me with their phone calls, they'll find out that I am different from the swine they are used to dealing with!" He started angrily for the door.

"Where are you going?" Luke asked.

He turned and looked back at her. "Downstairs to see that Ileana gets to the plane. Want to come along?"

She shook her head. "No, thanks," she said. "I can

live without saying good-bye to your lady friend." She reached for a drink as he went out the door.

He was smiling as he came out of the Italian Airlines Building and started for the parking lot where he had left his car. Ileana would do all right. He didn't have to worry about her. The message would be delivered.

Still there was something about her. Who else but Ileana would keep her eyes open for opportunity at a time like this? He almost laughed to himself at the way she found that young man. It was the white Stetson hat. Of course, he turned out to be a rich Texan. That young man would be a lot poorer before the flight was over.

He stepped into the parking lot and began to walk down the row of cars. It was late and there were not too many cars about. The sound of footsteps keeping time with his own came to him. He stopped for a moment and looked back.

There was no one there. He shrugged his shoulders and began to walk again. Again he heard the footsteps. He paused to light a cigarette. The footsteps stopped also. The cigarette lit, he began to walk again.

A moment later he heard the footsteps. They were heavy and deliberate. This time he was sure they were following him. He slowed his pace to see if the footsteps would keep time with him. They did.

He was almost at his car now. He let the stiletto slide into his hand. The cold feel of the metal was reassuring. He stepped between two cars and whirled suddenly, the knife pointed outward in his hand.

STILETTO

"Who's there?" His voice echoed strangely in the empty parking lot.

There was no answer. He waited a moment. The lot was silent. It had been nothing but the echoes of his own footsteps that he had heard. He let the stiletto slide back into its sheath. He was letting that stupid telephone call disturb him. He laughed to himself, feeling the tension drain from him as he got into the car.

He switched on the motor. He felt the faint prickling in his loins as he always did after a moment of danger. He thought of Luke waiting in the apartment. He was glad she would be there tonight. He needed someone like her. She would help him to rest.

He put the Alfa-Romeo into gear and started out of the lot. He knew the type of woman Luke was but she was not the kind who went with every man. She was motivated by identification. And when she found what she sought it was like a magic key to her own body and she could no longer control her desires.

Then would come the struggle to assert her superiority. First, sexually, by demands that would grow beyond the limits of fulfillment. He smiled to himself. That was the stage she was at right now. After that would come the others, the insistence upon acceptance as equal to the male in work and achievement, then superiority to the male by virtue of her femininity.

That she would never achieve. Not with him nor with anyone who would attract her, for she was not drawn to weaklings. For them she only had contempt. And the last stage in the pattern was her demand for rejection which came last. This she would always achieve.

For this was the stone on which she cleansed herself and absolved her conscience so that she might go forward and repeat the pattern of her life. So it would not be too difficult when this was over for him to do what he had to do. In a way it was of her own seeking. By that time he would be ready too. He would have had his fill and become bored with her.

And Ileana would be back by then. He thought of her with a smile. Maybe they would marry. It was time to think of carrying on the name. The blood lines would be good together and Ileana was European.

Europeans were much more honest than Americans, much more realistic. Compared with the complexities of Luke, Ileana seemed as simple and as direct as a schoolgirl.

24

"Well, it's been two days," Strang said. "How do you think we're doin'?"

Baker shrugged his shoulders. "It's anybody's guess. He picks up the phone now and disconnects before we get halfway through." He took out a cigarette and lit it. "What do your men in the field have to say?"

"I've switched them about six times already," Strang answered. "They say he's beginning to get jumpy. The usual things. Looking back over his shoulder, checking doorways before he goes in and out of them."

"And the girl?" Baker asked. "What about her?"

"She seems in better shape than he is," Strang said. "She's always with him but maybe she doesn't know what's going on."

"I've got the report on her," Baker said. "She seems pretty straight. She is a racing-car driver. Pretty good too, from what we can tell. Had some hard luck and lost her own car last year and she's saving up to get another one now."

"That isn't much help," Strang said. "It doesn't explain her willingness to alibi him for what happened out in the Mexican desert."

"She seems to want a car pretty bad," Baker said. "He's the boy who can give her one."

"Not just now, he isn't," Strang said. "We just found out that his car franchises were canceled."

"All of them?" Baker asked.

Strang nodded. "All of them. I wonder if that means anything."

"It might," Baker answered. "I'll have it checked out." The telephone rang. He picked it up. "It's for you," he said, giving the telephone to Strang.

Strang took it and listened for a moment, then put down the phone. "That was one of my men. Cardinali and the girl just went into the Pavillon on 57th Street for lunch."

Baker smiled and picked up the telephone. "It's about time for another call," he said to Strang. "Call Mr. Cardinali at the Pavillon restaurant and play the recording for him again," he said into it.

"I tell you I saw that man following us," Cesare insisted. "I recognized him. I saw him before."

Luke looked at him. "Are you sure, Cesare? I didn't see anyone."

"He was around the corner on Park Avenue by that time. I am sure." Cesare fell quiet as the waiter brought their drinks.

They sipped at their cocktails silently until the

waiter left. Luke put her hand on his arm. "What you need is some rest," she said softly. "You didn't get any sleep at all last night."

"Who can sleep with that telephone ringing?" Cesare said irritably. "There were four calls before we finally left the receiver off the hook."

"I'd have the phone shut off," Luke said.

"And admit to them that they have upset me?" Cesare said. "That is what they would like."

The waiter came back to the table. He was carrying a telephone with him. "There is a call for Count Cardinali." He bowed.

Cesare looked at Luke. "All right, I'll take it," he said to the waiter.

The waiter bowed again and plugged it into a jack behind them on the banquette. Cesare took the phone from him. "Cardinali speaking," he said into it.

Luke could see his face harden as he listened. He put down the telephone silently. He nodded in answer to the question on her face.

"Again," he said heavily, picking up his drink. "You see, we were being followed. They knew just where to call me."

The telephone began to ring just as they entered the apartment. Tonio hurried by them to pick it up. "Count Cardinali's residence," he said into it. He looked up at them. "Just a moment I will see if he's in."

He put down the telephone and came over to them. "There is a call for you, Excellency, but the signor will not give his name. He says only that he has an important message for you."

"I'll take it," Cesare said, crossing to the phone. He listened silently as Tonio hurried from the room. Suddenly his face contorted with anger and he ripped the telephone from its socket and flung it across the room.

"Damned instrument of torture!" he snapped as it crashed into a vase. He flung himself down on the couch as Tonio came hurrying into the room, a look of fright on his round little face.

"Clean up that mess!" Cesare snapped at him.

"Yes, Excellency! Immediately, Excellency!" the little man answered and hurried from the room.

Cesare leaned forward and placed his head in his hands. Luke went around behind him and massaged the back of his neck sympathetically.

"Take it easy," she said. "That won't do any good. I'll fix you a drink."

She walked over to the liquor cabinet and took down the gin and vermouth. Quickly she stirred a martini and poured it. She looked around for the bitters. Europeans liked a dash of bitters in their martinis.

It wasn't on any of the open shelves. She turned the key on the small door at the rear of the cabinet. A lone small dark bottle stood there. She took it out and turned toward him. "A dash of bitters?" she asked.

He was staring at her hand. "Where did you get that?" he snapped.

She gestured with her hand. "From here. I know you like . . ."

"Put it back," he said sharply. "And stay out of locked doors."

"You don't have to take my head off," she retorted angrily, putting the bottle back and closing the door.

He relaxed slightly. "I'm sorry, darling," he apologized. "The bitters are on the shelf below the bar."

"What's in that bottle anyway?" she asked, handing him the drink.

He sipped the drink and looked up at her. "Poison. Unfortunately I can't hang it on the wall like the other weapons," he said. "I got it from a chemist in Florence who was doing research on the poisons Lucrezia Borgia used. A few drops and there's no antidote. He said their knowledge of chemistry was fantastic for their times."

She looked over at the cabinet curiously. "I wouldn't feel safe having it around."

He finished the drink. "It's safe enough there. Nobody ever opens that door, even to clean it." He leaned his head back against the couch and closed his eyes. "I'm so tired," he said.

She stroked his forehead. "I know, lover," she said gently. "If there were only some place we could go, some place where nobody could find us until Ileana got back."

He turned around suddenly and looked up at her. The tension was disappearing from his face and he began to smile. "That's it!" he exclaimed. "Why didn't I think of it? I know just the place. They will never think of looking for us there!"

She smiled down at him. A warmth began to spread inside her. The time was only beginning, she thought proudly, when he would learn how necessary she was to him.

Detective Sergeant McGowan looked at his watch. It was almost eleven o'clock. One more hour until his relief would show up. He stamped his feet in the cold night air. That was the only lousy thing about this job. He had been waiting outside the hotel since four this afternoon.

Still it wasn't too bad. At least they didn't have to try to remain invisible like they did on some jobs. That was one of the big jokes in the trade. On television one lone private eye shadowed a suspect right into his bedroom and was never spotted. In real life it was a little different. The captain had six men on this job. There was one man at every entrance to the big hotel and two men constantly circling the block in a car to maintain contact and lend a hand if they were needed.

The car had just turned the corner at Lexington away from him when he glanced back at the hotel entrance and they came out.

The girl was carrying a small valise, the man looked up and down the street quickly and, waving away a taxi, took her arm. They started walking rapidly toward Lexington.

McGowan started after them. Just his luck they would pick this time to make a break. Now he wouldn't get home before six in the morning.

They cut across the street at the corner and headed up toward 51st Street. He cut in behind them and saw the man look back. He didn't try to hide himself. He didn't have to on this job. They turned the corner and went down into the subway entrance.

He broke into a run now and reached the top of the subway steps just as the roar of an entering train came to him. He took the steps down two at a time. The captain wouldn't like it if he were to lose them.

He caught a glimpse of a shadow out of the corner of his eye as he darted around the corner at the bottom of the stairway. He half turned to see the flat upraised hand of the man coming down on him in a vicious judo chop. He tried to roll away from it when the pain exploded in his shoulder and he sank to his knees.

He wasn't all the way out but there were lights flashing in his eyes and ringing sounds in his brain. That was like it was on TV, he remembered thinking vaguely. He shook his head. His vision began to clear.

He put his hand against the wall and pushed himself to his feet. He stood there dizzily for a moment, his eyes peering down to the platform.

He saw them getting on the train and started toward the platform after them. Before he reached the turnstiles, the doors had closed and the train began to pull out. He saw the man's face through the window, looking back at him. He was smiling.

Wearily he turned and headed for the telephone booth. He sank into it and heard the dime go tinkling down the box. The captain wouldn't like to hear they had gotten away but the captain should have told him the guy could hit like that. He began to dial the number.

Strang put down the telephone. He stared at Baker. "The plan worked all right," he said grimly. "But it worked too good. He cold-cocked McGowan on a subway platform and got away from him."

"The girl too?" Baker asked.

Strang nodded. "Yes."

Baker reached for a cigarette. His fingers were

trembling. "Heaven help them if the mob finds them before we do," he said.

"If they do, better have your resignation typed," Strang said heavily. "Mine's already in my top desk drawer!"

25

There are few places in New York that are resisting the advance of modern low-cost housing aid as successfully as upper Park Avenue. One of the reasons is that this is the shopping mecca of Spanish Harlem. Here below the tracks of the New York Central that speeds the commuter safely to his tiny surburban comfort is one of the last open markets of the city.

The people who shop here are mostly of Puerto Rican descent and they thread their way in their gaily-colored clothing among the pushcarts and sidewalk display, chattering as lightly and as happily, despite their poverty, as they did at home in their tropical island. There are hotels in this section of Park Avenue also. They do not much resemble the hotels farther downtown on the same avenue but they accomplish the same purpose. They are a place to sleep and eat and offer solace to a weary traveler. The main difference between the hotels in addition to the furnishings is the credit card. In Spanish Harlem the hotels are only interested in cash.

Cesare turned back from the window of the Del Rio Hotel as a train shot past them on the tracks outside. He looked at Luke who was seated in a chair, the morning newspapers in front of her. He lit a cigarette. "Isn't there something else you can do besides read the damn newspapers all day?"

Luke looked up at him. The whole of the last week he had been on edge. Nervous and irritable. It had been more than two weeks since Ileana had left and they had remained cooped up in this room most of that time.

At first it had been fun. They had laughed at all the little inconveniences: the dripping faucet, the squeaking bed, the sagging chairs. Then bit by bit the tawdry room seemed to creep into them until one morning it was no longer fun.

She was aware of what was coming but he had not been. Women were much more adaptable than men. They had a great deal more patience. They were better equipped for waiting. All the way around, mentally as well as physically. She remembered that she had felt a twinge of pain that usually accompanied the onslaught of her period. But nothing had happened. Idly she wondered if she were pregnant. It was more than a week now and she was rarely that late.

"Why don't you lie down and get some rest?" she suggested patiently.

He turned on her savagely. "Rest? That's all I've been getting in this stinking hole! Eating greasy food and sleeping in that dirty bed! I'm sick of it!"

"It's better than being dead," she said.

"Sometimes I wonder," he snapped, walking back to the window and looking down at the street.

She turned back to the newspaper but his voice came to her from the window and she looked up at him. He was still looking out.

"I used to see people like those down there in the village in Italy when I was a little boy. Look at them. Smiling, shouting as they scratch around in the rubble for something to eat."

She got out of her chair and joined him at the window. "They seem perfectly happy to me," she said, looking down.

Cesare's voice was wondering. "That is what I never could understand. What makes them so happy all the time? What have they got that we have not? Don't they know this world is for the few who take? They must know this. And still they are content to smile and laugh and make babies. What is it they have, that we have not?"

She looked up at him. She remembered when she had been a little girl. The excitement of going into town on shopping days. Poor Cesare, there were so many things he had never had. "Maybe they have hope," she said.

He looked down at her. "Hope?" He laughed. "That is a word invented by dreamers."

She wanted him to understand. "Maybe they have faith."

He laughed again. "That is a word invented by priests."

She couldn't keep her hand from his bare arm. Maybe the knowledge would flow from her touch into

235

him. The way she felt. "Maybe they have love," she said softly.

He stared down at her, then turned, pulling his arm from her touch. "That word is the biggest fraud of them all. It is a word invented by women to mask their biological needs and duties. Love, hah!"

She walked back to her chair and sat down. She picked up the newspapers but she did not really see them. There was a strangely familiar hurt aching inside her. "Maybe I don't know then."

He came over from the window and stared down at her. She didn't have to look up to know the cruel smile on his lips. She had seen it often enough in the last few days. Each time he turned from her, from the desperate need for him inside her.

"That is right," he said. "You don't know. The truth is that nobody knows. But I am the only one who admits it. There is nothing more to men than the desire to exist. And most of them don't really care how. Just exist. Day to day. Year to year. For nothing."

She was just about to answer him when there was a knock at the door. When she looked up, there was a stiletto in his hand. "Yes?" she called.

The porter's voice came through the door. "I have the afternoon papers, ma'am."

"Leave them at the door," she called. "I'll get them in a minute."

"Yes, ma'am," the voice called back. They waited a moment until they heard the footsteps go down the hall.

She got out of her chair and walked over to the door. Quickly she opened it, pulled the papers inside and closed the door again. She took them back to her chair and sat down. She began to open one of them.

He knocked the paper viciously from her hand. "Will you never stop reading those damn newspapers?" He walked back to the window.

Patiently she bent over to pick them up when she saw the picture. "Cesare, Cesare!" she cried, holding the paper toward him. "Look! She's back!"

There on the photo page of the *Journal-American* was a picture of Ileana, smiling and waving at the camera from the ramp of an airliner. The caption over the picture was simple: *Baroness Returns From Holiday Abroad.*

The group of men in Baker's office leaned forward tensely as Ileana's voice came through the speaker on his desk. "Hello," she said.

Cardinali's voice sounded strained and hurried. "This is Cesare. Have you got the message?"

One of the agents picked up another phone and whispered into it.

"Cesare, where are you? Are you all right?" Ileana's voice came from the speaker.

Baker looked up at the agent on the telephone. "She's stalling just as we told her. Are you on the trace?"

"We're moving as fast as we can, sir," the agent replied.

"I have it," Ileana said. "But Cesare, I don't understand it!"

"That doesn't matter," he snapped. "Tell me!"

Her voice was hesitant. "The moon will rise tonight."

A click came through the speaker as Cesare hung up, then Ileana's voice again. "Cesare! Cesare! Are you there?"

Baker looked up at the agent. "Did you pin him?"

The agent shook his head. "He went off too fast."

Ileana's voice came through the speaker again. "Cesare?"

Baker picked up the other telephone on his desk. "He's off the line, Baroness."

Her voice sounded frightened to him. "Did I do all right, Mr. Baker?" she asked. "I held him as long as I could."

"You did fine, Baroness," he said with a confidence he did not feel. "We've got everything under control."

He put down the telephone and looked up at the agent. "Thank you," he said to him. "You can knock off now."

"Surely there's something we can do if he comes out of hiding tomorrow," the agent said.

"What?" Baker asked.

"He did send the woman out of the country to get a message," the younger man said.

Baker smiled. "There's no law against that."

The agent shook his head and walked out of the office. Baker turned to Captain Strang who sat opposite him. Strang looked at him. "It was a good try, George," he said quietly.

Baker smiled wearily. "It wasn't good enough."

"You did everything you could," Strang said.

Baker got out of his chair. Failure tasted bitter in his mouth. He looked down at Strang. "Let's be honest about it, Dan," he said. "It's over." He walked to the window and looked out. "If Cardinali shows up tomorrow, it means the Stiletto will have gotten away with it. If he doesn't, well, we lose anyway. We're no closer to Matteo than we were before."

He turned back to the policeman, his voice was bitter. "They beat us, Dan. Either way, we lose."

26

They left the hotel about ten o'clock at night. "It's not far from here," he told her as they began to walk. They turned off Park Avenue at 116th Street and headed for Madison. They made several turns more at different corners, then Cesare touched her arm.

"It's across the street," he said.

She looked. It was one of those old brownstone tenements that had a bar and grill in the basement floor. A small neon sign blinked on and off over the door. *The Quarter Moon Bar and Grill* it read in white and green letters.

He led her past the saloon entrance and up the steps of the house. The door was open and they walked into the hallway. A single naked bulb hung overhead and cast a dim yellow light.

She looked up at him. "Who are we going to see?" she asked.

He looked down at her. "Matteo, of course," he answered matter-of-factly.

"But I thought he couldn't enter this country," she said in surprise.

He smiled at her. "So do many others." He took her arm again. "Come."

They walked up one flight of stairs to the next floor. Cesare stopped in front of a door. He knocked on it.

"Come in. The door is unlocked." Matteo's voice came through it.

Cesare opened the door and they entered the room. She was surprised to see it was a comfortably furnished office. She did not expect it in a building such as this. Cesare closed the door behind him.

Matteo looked up at them from behind a desk. "Don Cesare! And Miss Nichols too. I am surprised."

Cesare left her standing at the door and walked over to the desk. He stood there looking down silently at Matteo.

Luke looked curiously around the room. It was just like a regular business office. There was another desk in the corner with a typewriter on it. Next to it was a file cabinet and next to that was a small curtained alcove that probably led to the lavatory. The only thing strange about the room was that there seemed to be no windows in it. Matteo's voice came to her and she looked back at them.

"You have asked for a meeting, my nephew," he said.

Cesare nodded. "I have come to talk to you about a misunderstanding between us."

"Yes?" Emilio inclined his head.

"When we last met, you said to me that I have done my work well. That the Society was pleased." Cesare's voice was low.

Emilio nodded. "That is true."

"Then why is it they ask my death?" Cesare asked calmly.

Emilio folded his hands across his stomach and leaned back in the chair. He looked up at Cesare. "You are young, my nephew, and there are many things you do not understand."

"What things?" Cesare asked.

"The Society owes its existence to one simple rule," Emilio said blandly. "One simple rule that helped it survive many wars and many difficult times of strife and built it to the power it is today. And this rule is our strength. 'No one man can exist who threatens the security of more than himself.' "

"I have not broken this rule," Cesare said quickly. "Except at the request of the Society to protect certain of its members."

Emilio's voice was still patient as if he were speaking to a child. "It is regrettable, of course, but that knowledge is now a dagger at our throats. You see, already the police suspect you and if somehow your knowledge should become available to them—" He didn't finish his sentence.

"They will discover nothing from me," Cesare said.

"I believe that," Emilio agreed. "But vast harm would be done if we both are in error. The others have not the same confidence as you and I."

"Why not?" Cesare demanded. "I have kept the oath. And I want nothing from them."

"That's just it," Emilio said quickly. "That is what

243

concerns them. A man who wants nothing has nothing to protect. You are not like Dandy Nick, or Big Dutch and Allie whom you have already eliminated. They had reason to be loyal, they had something to protect, profits to contribute. While you, my nephew, bring us no profit, produce nothing. You are a dilettante, interested only in the excitement and danger like a little child."

"So, because of Dandy Nick, they ask my death?" Cesare asked.

Emilio looked up at him. He held his hands apart expressively in gesture of helplessness. "For that reason you must keep your oath to the society."

Luke saw a movement behind the curtain. "Cesare! Look out!" she screamed in sudden terror.

Cesare whirled so quickly that her eye did not follow the stiletto flying from his hand. It plunged into the curtain and into the man hidden behind it in the alcove. The man's hands gripped the curtain and fell with it to the floor, ripping it from its hanger. A gun fell clattering to the floor near Luke.

Cesare knelt quickly by the man, pulling the curtain from his face. He looked back at Emilio. "It is Dandy Nick!" he said harshly. "Now according to the law there is no one I threaten!"

"There is still one, my nephew," Emilio said softly.

Cesare stared up at him. "Who is that, my uncle?"

The gun appeared in Emilio's hand. "Me," he said quietly. His finger began to tighten on the trigger. In a way, it was a shame, he thought almost regretfully. Cesare could have become one of the great ones, one of the Dons, but there was something missing.

He was so lost in his reverie that he did not see

Luke squeeze the trigger of the gun she had picked up from the floor. The impact of the bullet in his shoulder tumbled him backward from his chair, the gun flying from his hand.

In a moment, Cesare was upon him, the stiletto high in the air over his head. "No! No!" Matteo screamed. "I will speak to the council! They will listen to me!"

Cesare was laughing wildly now. "It is too late, my uncle!" he shouted. "Their own rules condemn you! With your death, I am free!"

Luke watched, frozen in horror, as the knife came down again and again into Emilio's body. "Stop, Cesare!" she screamed. "It's enough!"

Slowly Cesare rose from behind the desk. He turned toward her, the wild maniacal light beginning to fade from his eyes. He was smiling by the time he reached her. He took her arm and opened the door.

He looked back into the room and then down at her. "You know," he said softly with a laugh, "he was beginning to believe he really was my uncle!"

He opened the door of his apartment and they went inside. He crossed to his desk and sat down. He pushed aside the stack of mail and took out a check book and began to write in it.

Luke came up behind him and gently began to massage the back of his neck. "It's good to be home," she said softly.

He finished writing the check and turned around, holding it up to her. "Here!" he said harshly.

She stopped massaging his neck and stared down at him. "What's that for?" she asked.

His voice was flat and his eyes were the eyes of a

stranger. "You said you wanted a Ferrari. Now you can pack your things and go!"

She stared at him, unbelieving. There was a sickness in her stomach, a nausea that was creeping up in her. It was happening again. The same thing was happening again! "You think—" Her voice choked for a moment. She could taste the bitter bile from her stomach. "You think that is why I stayed with you?"

He got out of the chair and walked roughly past her to the liquor cabinet. He poured himself a drink and swallowed it. He turned back to her. "It doesn't matter what I think," he said. "We are finished!"

She had to tell him. Maybe if he knew she was pregnant, he wouldn't feel like that. It wasn't his fault. He had been through so much. "Cesare, what am I going to do now? I am . . . I don't . . ."

He reached behind him in the cabinet, opened the little door and took out the small dark bottle. He placed it on the cabinet near the whisky. "I don't care what you do," he interrupted her. "But you have a choice. You know what is in this bottle. A few drops and in three minutes—oblivion! Very painless. I give it to you!"

He walked past her to the door. She followed him. "Cesare!" she cried. "Where are you going? To her?"

He smiled slowly, his voice was cruelly soft. "Yes. I am tired of you. I've had enough of lying with you on coarse bleach-smelling sheets, of your plebeian attempts at love-making! You were right in what you said the first time we met. She can give me more in ten minutes than you can in ten days. And you've just proved it!"

246

STILETTO

Her hand reached for his lapel. "You don't want me any more?" she asked dully.

He brushed her hand away. "That's not quite right," he said coldly. "I don't need you any more!"

The door closed behind him and she stood there for a moment staring at it. Then she turned and slowly walked back to the couch. It had happened again. She looked over at the vial of poison standing on the edge of the liquor cabinet. He was right. It was the only way for someone like her.

She got to her feet and started for it when the nausea came up in her. She ran to the bathroom wildly and bent over the sink, retching. Tears began to burn in her eyes. She retched again and then her stomach was empty. Slowly she sank to her knees and placed her head against the cool porcelain. The tears came rolling down her cheeks. There was no doubt about it now.

27

He turned the key in Ileana's door and walked into the room. The lights were on and he could hear the sound of the water running in the shower. He smiled and walked over to the bathroom door and called to her. "Ileana!"

He heard the water stop, then her voice. "Cesare! Is that you?"

"Yes." He laughed. "I'm back."

"Are you all right?" she asked.

"I'm fine," he called. "Hurry out. I have something important to tell you!"

He turned from the door. It was time for them. The time for adventure was over and the time for family had begun. He knew now what his father had meant when he said to him, "Do not let the name die, my son. Take care not to waste all your seed."

249

He heard her call through the door. "Be a dear, will you, and hand my makeup case in through the door to me? It will never do for you to see me without lipstick. It's on the night table."

He laughed to himself, thinking of all the times he had seen her without lipstick. But he might as well get used to her little vanities. It would be a part of their life together.

He walked over to the night table and picked up the small case by the handle. The snaps were open and the case opened outward, the lower half spilling its contents on the floor. Still smiling, he knelt to pick them up. He tumbled the lipsticks and the compacts back into the case and began to pick up the cards and letters still on the floor.

Idly he looked at them. What junk a woman carried. Credit cards and charge plates. The last letter caught his eye. It was marked, *Official Business U. S. Government*. It was addressed to Ileana from the Department of Immigration. Automatically he began to read it.

"At the request of Mr. George Baker of the Federal Bureau of Investigation we herewith advise you that your request for a visa as a permanent resident alien has been approved. Please bring this letter and your passport to our nearest office so that proper entry may be made accordingly."

Slowly Cesare got to his feet, the letter still in his hand, the makeup case forgotten on the floor. He had opened the bathroom door before he fully understood what the letter meant. She had been working for Baker all the time. There could be no other reason for him to help her.

She was standing before the mirror tying her robe around her. She looked up into it and saw him. She spun around swiftly at the expression on his face. "Cesare! What is wrong?" she cried. Then she saw the letter in his hand. Her eyes widened.

He stood there in the doorway, his eyes cold and dead. "Why, Ileana, why? You came to me as a friend for help and I helped you. Why?"

She stared up at him. "I had to, Cesare. They gave me no choice!"

"I don't believe that, Ileana," he said, walking toward her. "You still could have told me. We could have fought this together."

She watched him raise his hand slowly. Oddly enough she wasn't afraid now that it was happening. She wondered if the others had felt the same way. "Don't do it, Cesare," she said calmly. "You can't get away with it now. They'll know it was you."

He stared down at her, his hand hesitating.

"Don't, Cesare," she said quickly, trying to take advantage of his hesitation. "You're sick. Let me help you!"

"You've helped enough," he said bitterly. "I was even fool enough to think of marrying you!"

She tried to dart past him to the door and never saw the blow that tumbled her unconscious to the floor.

He stood there looking down at her, breathing heavily. His mind raced. He dared not use the stiletto. There had to be a way to make it look like an accident.

As he did with Barbara. He opened the bathroom

251

door and looked out into the bedroom. He saw the french doors leading to the terrace. The idea crystallized in his mind. A suicide was even better.

He picked her up swiftly and carried her to the terrace doors. He opened them and looked out. The night was silent and the snow had started to fall in big white flakes. He stepped out onto the terrace and carried her to the parapet. He placed her limp body on it for a moment and looked at her.

Her face was white and still and small. Somewhere in his mind he could hear the sound of her tinkling laughter. She would have made a lovely bride for him. He touched her lightly and she rolled over and was gone.

He did not stop to look down after her. He turned and hurried back into the room and out into the hall.

He came back into his living room and walked toward the couch. He stopped as Luke came to the bedroom door. "You still here?" he snapped.

She didn't answer.

He turned from her and sank into the couch. "What are you waiting for?" he almost shouted. "Get out!"

He leaned forward and placed his head in his hands. He rubbed his neck wearily. Luke walked over to the liquor cabinet and poured a drink into his glass.

She came around in front of him and held it out. "Here," she said.

He took it and swallowed the whisky in one gulp. He put the glass down on the table before him and looked up at her. "Now get your things and go," he said harshly.

252

Silently she turned and went into the bedroom. He leaned his head back against the couch wearily. He was so tired. Tomorrow he would go away somewhere and do nothing but lie in the sun. He closed his eyes. It had been such a long time since he had been in the sun. He started to get to his feet. He might as well go to bed.

He brought his head forward but something had gone wrong. It was as if his feet had gone to sleep. He pushed himself from the couch but that didn't help either, there was no strength in his arms.

Luke came out of the bedroom, carrying her valise. She walked by him without speaking.

He felt the perspiration break out on his forehead. "Luke! Help me," he called. "I feel strange!"

She turned to look at him. "I can't help you now, Cesare," she said in a low voice.

He stared at her for a moment, then he looked at the empty liquor glass on the table before him. Suddenly comprehension came to him. "You bitch! You've poisoned me!" he shouted. "I should have killed you in the desert!"

"Maybe you should have," she said unemotionally. "I told you I never wanted to be a loser again." She turned to the door and opened it.

Baker and several men stood there. They pushed her back into the room with them. Baker looked down at him. He turned to Luke. "What's the matter with him?" he asked.

A vague memory stirred through Cesare's mind. He stared up at them, his face tightening.

"He's dying," Luke said.

"Lucrezia!" Cesare suddenly screamed.

Baker sprang into action. "Get a doctor up here!" he snapped to one of the men.

"It's too late for that." Luke began to laugh. "The only thing that will help him is a priest!"

"Get a doctor anyway," Baker said quickly. "And get her out of here!"

Strang came into the room as Luke and the agent went out. "The Baroness will be okay," he said. "She'll have to stay in bed for a few days but there are no bones broken!"

Cesare looked up at them. "But Ileana is dead!"

Baker shook his head. "Her terrace was on a set-back. She only fell one flight. And that was broken by an awning."

Cesare began to laugh.

Strang looked at Baker. "What's the matter with him?" he asked.

"He's dying," Baker said. "He took poison!"

Cesare looked up at them. That was the biggest joke of all. The fools should know that the Borgias did not poison themselves. For a moment he almost told them what had really happened, then he kept it inside him. Let it be one more thing the stupid *carabinieri* would never find out. He laughed again.

Baker leaned over him. "Where are Matteo and Dandy Nick?" he asked.

Cesare looked up at him. He was smiling. "Dead. They are all dead."

"Why did you do it, Cardinali? Why?" Baker asked quickly. "You never wanted what they did. You had everything going for you."

Cesare tried to focus his eyes on Baker's face. It was

blurring in front of him. "My father used to say that too, Mr. Baker, but the only reason he took me into the house was to carry on the name. And I don't know whether you would understand it either. There are only two things in life that mean anything. Birth and death. Everything else in between—living—is nothing. Empty."

He paused to catch his breath. "It is only when you dip your hands into these that a man is really alive. That's why you go inside a woman. To be born again. That's why you stand there watching me die, sharing the excitement of my death. You feel more alive this moment than you ever felt before!" He leaned his head back against the couch, the perspiration running down his face in rivulets.

"The man's mad!" Strang said hoarsely, his face white. "Stark, raving mad!"

Cesare raised his head to look at the policeman. It was taking all his strength just to see through the veil that was falling in front of him. In the distance he could hear the sound of an infant crying. Maybe the man was right. Maybe he was mad. What was a new-born baby doing, crying in a place like this? Suddenly the knowledge came to him. It was his child that was crying. That was what Luke had tried to tell him. She was carrying his child within her.

He called up all his strength to find his voice. He could feel his lips twist in an agony of effort. "Isn't the . . . whole world . . . a little . . . mad?" he asked as the veil dropped down, taking them away from him.